THE GENESI CODE

The Genesi Code by Tristen Willis
Published by Tristen Willis
© All rights reserved

1ˢᵗ Edition 2017, paperback.
ISBN: 978-1-925635-46-1

Publishing services by: Australian eBook Publisher
www.AustralianEbookPublisher.com.au

Designer: Sharnai James-McGovern, Australian eBook Publisher

National Library of Australia Cataloguing-in-Publication entry
Creator: Willis, Tristen, author.
Title: The Genesi code / Tristen Willis.
ISBN: 9781925635461 (paperback)
ISBN: 9781925635447 (epub)
Series: Willis, Tristen. Genesi series ; 1.
Subjects: Genetic engineering--Fiction.
                 Murder--Fiction.
                 Science fiction.

Also available as an ebook from major ebook vendors.

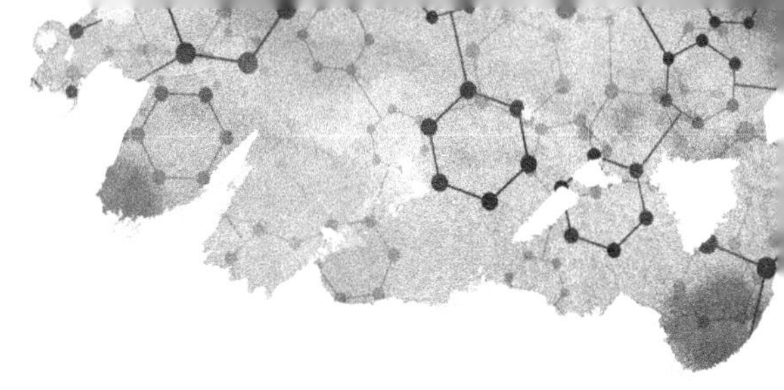

THE GENESI CODE

Book One of The Genesi Series

TRISTEN WILLIS

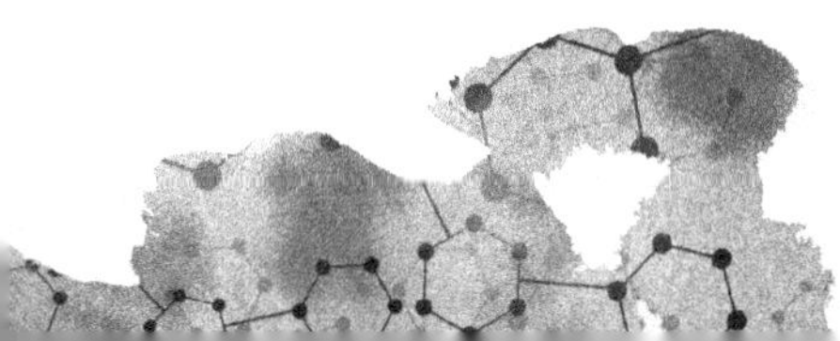

To my partner and my family,
for always encouraging me to try.

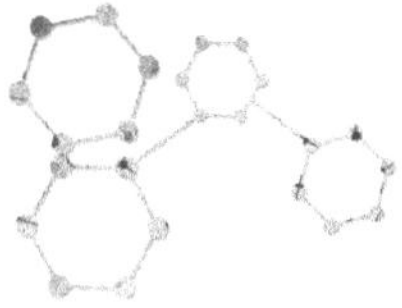

PROLOGUE

THE STREETS ARE quiet and deserted as I make my way across the city under the cover of darkness.

I listen for footsteps and other stirring noises; so far, I have not sensed any pursuers, but that does little to settle the unease I feel. I know that it's only a matter of time before they figure out what I have discovered. I am not safe anymore, nor is my family. Soon, they will come for me.

The streets are still quiet as I make my way to my parked car, keeping as close to the shadows as possible. The car unlocks as I approach and I cast one last glance around the street before I climb into the driver's seat, locking the doors behind me. The engine ignites with a soft purr and I ease the car out of the park. Soon, I am driving through the dark and deserted streets of the city relieved there are no cars following me.

When I reach the long driveway leading to my home, I slow the car to a stop, searching for signs of imminent danger. There is nothing lurking in the shadows of trees lining the drive, but that does not mean no one is there.

I ease my foot onto the gas and make my way down the drive. As I approach the manor house, I notice that everything appears normal. The inside of the house is dark—my family still asleep.

The sensor light detects the movement of the car and turns on, drowning me in a flood of bright light. I look up to the porch, checking that no one is waiting for me before climbing out and walking up the steps.

I hesitate at the front door, listening for any sounds of disturbance before unlocking it and stepping inside as quietly as possible. I am greeted with dead silence. I run my right hand along the wall, feeling for the light switch, *there*, and turn them on.

I turn left and hurry silently down the hall towards my office, turning more lights on as I go. I reach the door at the end of the hallway and hesitate, listening for any sounds that might show someone could be on the other side of the door. I count a full minute in my head before opening it as silently as possible. The light from the hall is enough to tell me the room is empty. I turn the lights on and close the door, lock it behind me and breathe in a sigh of relief.

I take a good look at my office. The walls are lined with oak bookshelves from floor to ceiling and filled with an assortment of medical and scientific textbooks and encyclopaedias, with my desk over at the far wall. Made of a rich mahogany oak, it is covered in more textbooks and paperwork.

I sit down in the high back chair and switch the computer on. I type in my encrypted password and turn on its camera. I face myself in profile on the screen and hesitate. What am I supposed to say to her?

The truth.

I clear my throat and begin speaking into the camera.

'Luka,' I address the camera, my voice wavers only slightly as I try to compose myself. 'As you already know,

World War IV occurred in the year 2120. When the Genesi Code was created. It is known as the Genesi War.' My voice hitches slightly and I hesitate. 'What I am about to tell you, the truth is that they never wanted us to discover.' I take a deep breath to steady myself. Steeling my resolve, I address the camera once more.

'You see, Luka, for the Genesi Code to successfully adhere to the draft subject, they have to *die* in order for the process to be completed. If the draft subject did not die with the Genesi Coding in their system, it would lie dormant in the human body. I *need* you to understand that perfectly.'

'For years, scientists have been working on a way to reverse the biological damages caused by the Genesi coding. They believed that if the Genesi could be cured, or at least, turned back into humans, then the world would become safe again and we would no longer have to live inside our walls. Five years ago, I was hired by the senate to help them in their efforts. After two years with little result, I was pulled aside by Chancellor Cain and asked to work on a classified project.

'Chancellor Cain wanted me to re-create the Genesi coding, but altering it slightly so that those changed by the Genesi Coding would become susceptible to suggestion, so that they could be controlled. At first, I refused. Why would creating more Genesi help our cause? After my refusal, he threatened you and your mother. I saw no alternative but to do what he asked of me.'

'Now, Luka, I need you to pay very close attention to what I am about to tell you. What I am about to say is going to change everything...'

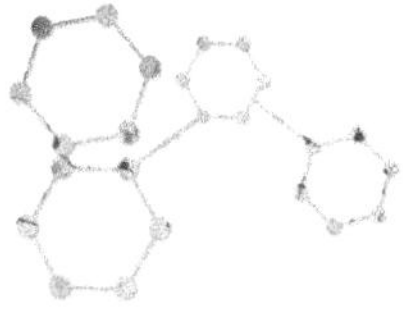

ONE

YEAR 2258

I LOUNGE ON the armchair inside my father's office, my legs dangling over its arm. My father sits at his desk, typing on the computer, intently focused on the work before him. The desk is made of a rich mahogany oak and is covered in stacks of papers and textbooks. I study the lines of his face, the way his brow creases in concentration, and how every now and then, he would lick his lips without even realising he was doing it. He has this habit of licking his lips when he finds something interesting in his work. I smile in amusement. He is tall and lean, with dirty blonde hair that is always cut short. He wears glasses when he is working; they have horn-rims and make him look older than he is by at least ten years. Or maybe it's the permanent dark circles under his eyes.

He looks up then, noticing my gaze. 'What are you looking at, Luka?' he asks me, and the corners of his mouth turn upwards in a smile. I try to answer him, but no sounds come out. I try again, but there is still no sound, and I begin to panic. I look at my father and try to speak again, only for soundless words to escape my lips. My father does not look worried at all that I have suddenly lost the ability to speak; instead, he speaks to me again. 'Everything is going to change.'

I wake to the blearing sound of my alarm. Without

opening my eyes, I stretch out my arm, blindly feeling until I find the 'off' switch. Slowly, I open my eyes. The room is still dark, so I reach over and tap the lamp on the small table beside my bed. The lamp turns on, bathing my bedroom in its light and I climb out of bed. I walk over to the closet and grab my training clothes hanging from the door—I had laid them out the night before. Clothes in hand, I enter the small ensuite bathroom.

I slip off my pyjamas—an oversized t-shirt—and dress in my training clothes: black sweat pants, sports bra and light grey t-shirt. I pad over to the basin and slap some cold water on my face to wake me up. I look up in the mirror, and I barely recognise the girl staring back at me. The girl in the reflection has the same tanned skin, olive green eyes and ash blonde hair that I do. But this girl is no reflection of who I am on the *inside*. I do not think I can remember how to be the girl in the reflection anymore.

Sighing and pushing those thoughts aside, I reach over and grab my hairbrush, combing my long hair back into a neat ponytail before tying it up. I take one last look at the girl in the mirror. 'Today, everything is going to change. You need to be brave, Luka.'

I walk out of my bathroom and into the hall, then down the stairs to the front door. I stop only to put my shoes and socks on before heading out the front door and into the early hours of dawn. It is still mostly dark outside; the sun has not yet risen. I walk down the three steps leading from the porch and make my way up the long drive.

As I make my way to the top of the drive, I see a dark figure standing in the middle of the street. His arms are crossed, and his messy dark brown hair falls into his eyes.

'You took your time this morning, everything okay?' he asks.

No, I wanted to say. 'I just didn't sleep well, that's all,' I say instead.

'Me either. Let's just get going.'

'Couldn't agree more,' I reply, as we take off jogging down the street.

Harvey is my best friend. We have lived across the road from each other our whole lives. When I was ten, my father was murdered. Harvey had found me passed out on the floor in the entry of our house that day. He had looked so terrified when he told me that he had heard gunshots. Instinct told me something terrible had happened to my father. I was bleary eyed and my lungs felt like they were drowning in acid, but I stood up and ran down the hall to his office. What I found in his office that day, I will never forget. The office had been trashed. Books had been pulled off their shelves and thrown on the floor, the bookshelves had been pulled from the walls, the desk at the back of the room had been up-ended and my father's favourite chair had two of its legs broken off. And there, behind the desk, was my father on the floor. I ran towards him and stopped, falling to my knees. He was dead. Blood was pooled around his head where the bullet had entered his skull and his eyes had been closed, almost as if the person who had killed him cared enough to close his eyelids, making it look like he was simply in a deep sleep that he would never wake from.

I remember screaming out my father's name, grabbing hold of his shoulders and shaking him, telling him to wake up even though I knew it was pointless; he was long dead. I remember sobbing into my father's chest and holding his body in my arms until Harvey grabbed me from behind and pulled me into him, holding me. We stayed like that for hours before anyone found us.

My father was a scientist working on a cure for the Genesi Coding. When I was younger, he told me about the Genesi and about the war. He told me that the Genesi are a race of genetically modified human soldiers that were created over one hundred years ago, before the war. They were designed to be the ultimate soldier, but no one anticipated that they would become the superior species and try to annihilate the human race. Now they are in hiding, biding their time, while we remain trapped inside the walls that our ancestors built.

My father was the only scientist ever to come close to finding a cure for the Genesi Coding, something hundreds, if not thousands, of people had tried to accomplish before him. Scientists once believed it was possible to find a cure, a way to reverse the damage done to the Genesi and turn them back to humans. However, it has been more than one hundred years, and they are no closer.

So far, the only person who has come close to solving the century-old mystery was my father, but then he was murdered. I was there that day, but I don't remember what happened and who killed him. They say that when someone has been through something so traumatic, their mind tries to protect them from the memory of it by blocking those memories. At least, that's what the doctors and scientists kept telling me, but I do not think even they knew what was wrong with me and why I could not remember anything that happened on that particular day.

When the investigation began, I was no longer allowed inside the house. Harvey's father was kind enough to let my mother and I stay at their house in the meantime. Because he was the Captain of the Guard, he kept us updated with the progress of the investigation. My mother and I had not spoken a word to each other; she had closed in on herself, shutting me and everyone else out. She needed her space to grieve, as did I.

The day I found my father, Harvey and I made a promise to each other. We promised that we would do whatever it took to find my father's killer and bring him to justice. Harvey and I both had different ideas of what the word 'justice' meant, though. Harvey said there were other means of bringing someone to justice, which could be that we would hand him over to the police, and he would be locked away for life, or he would be given the death sentence. Harvey was a gentle soul and I could tell he didn't want this man's death on my conscience. For argument's sake, I agreed with him that we would hand my father's killer over to the authorities, but deep down, we both knew that I wouldn't. I wanted *revenge*, not justice.

Our jog this morning was more for sentimental reasons than for training purposes. Since my father's death ten years ago, Harvey and I had begun to train. Every day, we would push our bodies to their limits, but today, we didn't need to. Our normal routine would be to jog into the centre of the city, then spend the rest of the morning before school training self-defence, and then the afternoons after school, as well as the weekends training and studying, preparing ourselves for what was to come. Today, we won't be going to school. Today, we will find out if we have been accepted into the elite task force for the military known as Delta Force. To be considered for training in Delta Force, you have to score highly on an aptitude test. Once accepted, you are then sent to the military base and are put through a series of gruelling physical and mental tests, with the aim of weeding out the weakest. Of the one hundred soldiers considered, only approximately two in ten make it through the six-month long training course. Only those who pass the training become a member of Delta Force. They are then deployed into the field, outside the walls, to hunt the Genesi. To say I was nervous about today was an understatement.

As we begin our jog through the city, the sun begins to rise, illuminating the houses with its faint glow. As we jog through the residential suburbs of the city, I can see some houses illuminated from within. People would be getting up to start their day, heading to work or school.

I live in Capital City, one of eighteen remaining cities in what was once known as America. We now call our land the United Nations—after America, Canada and Mexico joined together to form one nation. Capital City houses the senate and our governing leader, Chancellor Cain, along with the people that Harvey and I called 'the aristocrats.' The aristocrats were the people that came from wealthy families before the war and were able to buy their way into the city. They live in big manor houses and do little to provide for the community. Those who are not from a wealthy family in this city live in what is called 'the poor district' by the aristocrats, but it's more just an area where the houses don't have more than five bedrooms—the horror. The people that live in these suburbs are the workers of this city, and are allowed to reside in this Capital City as long as they serve the aristocrats and the senate. Harvey and I both live among the aristocrats, but our families are an exception to the spoilt, uptight sophisticates that live around us. Both my parents had been scientists. However, since my father's death, my mother stopped researching and simply works at the medical centre, tending to the ill. I do not blame her for no longer wanting to be a scientist. The compensation we received after the murder helps to maintain our home.

We jog through the rest of my suburb and past the streets that marked the entry to the poor district. I cannot help but envy the people who live here. All of the houses in this suburb are all similarly built: standard four-bedroom homes made of brick, with a small lawn, and their closest neighbour directly next to them. Life just feels so much simpler. Sure, they are all overworked and underpaid, but they all look out for one another. There is a sense of community that you would never see among the aristocrats.

We continue through the streets, winding our way along our usual route. I keep thinking about what my life would have been like if I grew up in this suburb instead of my own. What kind of person would I have been if nobody knew me as Christopher Foster's daughter, the scientist that was murdered? They broadcasted the news of my father's death across all of the cities, I didn't attend the funeral.

I snap out of these thoughts as we round the next corner, which would bring us out of the residential area. We slow as we reach the gates. A cast-iron gate, three times my size, separates the residential area from the rest of the city. It serves as yet another safety precaution in this city. The gate is always manned by two police officers—just another safety precaution. In the mornings, the guards are Deputy Brad Sanderson and Deputy Samuel Hale. This morning is no different.

'Morning, Miss Foster and Mr Montgomery. Didn't expect to see you two out this morning,' says Brad as he takes note of our arrival.

'It's our last run before our graduation ceremony,' says Harvey. 'The last goodbye, so to speak.'

'Of course, you two are likely to get shipped out tomorrow if you get accepted. Enjoy your last day of freedom.' Brad chuckles as he opens the gates for us.

We wave goodbye as we jog on through the gates; I can hear the heavy iron closing behind us. We increase our speed.

I look over at Harvey, and I can't help but admire the sight of concentration and determination on his face. His strong jaw is set and his bright blue eyes are focused on our route. His t-shirt is already covered in a damp sweat.

Harvey looks over at me and notices my gaze. 'What?' he huffs.

'Nothing, I just can't help but notice how much of a sweat you have broken; I thought this was supposed to be a nice, leisurely jog…' I joke.

Harvey smiles and it lights up his whole face, reaching his eyes, 'It *is* a nice leisurely jog, for *you*, anyway. I have to work a lot harder to keep up with you, *remember*.'

That was true. Even though Harvey and I have trained together for the last five years, I have always managed to push myself further, and he has always struggled to keep up. We joke that it's because I have a stronger reason to win than he does, but deep down, I always wonder if it is something more than that.

We make our way past the school and I can't help but feel glad that our school days are behind us now. No more having to pretend that I don't hear what people are always whispering about me. How strange and unnatural I am. How I am too anti-social, a snob. I always hid how their words made me feel. I was glad to be rid of them.

We pass the medical centre and the hospital, and then the streets lined with small shops and businesses. We pass the playing fields and public pool, then continue past the library and community centre, eventually slowing to a stop when we near the city centre and reach the quad in front of town hall.

The quad is a considerable square of grass with a six-foot-tall white marble fountain in its centre. The fountain spurts water into a shallow round pool that has a white marble bench surrounding it. There are black oak trees planted in each corner of the quad, their dark green leaves providing shade with more benches underneath them. We walk over and collapse on the bench around the fountain. The slight spray of water coming from the fountain feels cool and re-freshing on my skin.

I look up at the town hall. It is an imposing, Victorian English style building, made of brick and stone, with wide steps reaching up to its front entry where a set of impos-ing doors provide entry inside. The building is outstretched with a high-reaching clock tower atop it. I watch the last few seconds tick by before the hands strike the hour and the clock begins its booming chime of the hour. Seven times, the sound echoes through the quad.

'Five more minutes, then we can go inside,' says Harvey, but I barely hear him over the bell's chiming. I continue to control my breathing as I gaze up at town hall. In just two hours, our future will be decided. I try to savour the last few moments of my adolescent life. I focus on the sounds around me: the fountain water running as it spurts and pours back into its pool; warblers and blackbirds chirp as they wake to the sunlight of a new day; and cars and busses, with their engines and blaring horns—people on their way to start their day. I sigh.

I turn to look over at Harvey; his eyes closed and wear the hint of a smile. 'I'm going to miss this,' he says quietly.

'What, the training?' I tease.

He smiles, as if laughing to himself. 'No, *this*.' He gestures at the quads scenery with his hand to indicate everything around him.

I know what he means. I'll miss it, too. The stillness of early morning as the city begins to wake is always so peaceful.

'Me, too.'

Knowing our few minutes of reprieve are over, we both stand, stretching out our sore limbs. We head towards the community centre.

'Are you nervous about today?' He asks me as we walk.

'What, specifically, would I be nervous about?' I ask dryly.

He rolls his eyes. 'I just mean, all our plans are riding on this, on getting in. Besides, I have much more to be nervous about than you.'

'So much confidence in yourself.'

'You know it's true; I could ruin all your plans.'

'Come on, don't say it like that.'

'Like what?'

'Like I made you do this; like you had no choice. You are just reminding me of how selfish I am on making you do this. That I'm a terrible friend.'

'Hey, you aren't *making* me do anything. Besides, selfish people don't know that they are being selfish, much less admit that they are selfish.'

'No, that's *crazy* people. Crazy people don't know that they are crazy, much less admit that they are.'

He rolls his eyes.

'You never answered me; are you nervous?'

'I know. I'm actually trying not to think about it.'

He doesn't ask any more questions after that, and we walk the last few metres to the community centre in silence before we head inside.

We continue down the foyer and past the front desk, then down the hall leading to the bathrooms. Harvey and I separate as we enter the gendered bathrooms. I quickly shower and dress, then head back towards the basin area. The walls around me are lined with mirrors.

I put my towel, dirty clothes and toiletries on the small

bench next to the basin. I take a long, measured look at myself in the mirror. I had picked a black, form-fitting dress that stopped above the knee. The neckline was modest, touching my collarbone, and the sleeves covered my shoulders. I pull out my hairbrush and begin combing my hair back; I pull it up and tie it in a ponytail. I then wrap the length of hair around my head until it forms a neat bun and pin it into place. I look myself over in the mirror. It'll do. I pinch my cheeks a few times to force some colour into them. Satisfied, I gather my things and pad back out to my locker.

I unlock the locker and throw my things back inside, grabbing the heels my mum had given me the day before— simple little black peep-toes. Mum had given them to me especially for today, even though she knows I never wear anything higher than the one-inch heel of a boot. In fact, I do not wear heels. *Ever.*

Sighing, I lean one hand against the locker to brace myself while I put the shoes on. They pinch around my toes and I can tell I'll have blisters. Luckily, I only have to wear them for a couple of hours. I turn and walk back out of the locker room and into the hall.

Harvey is waiting for me, and looks up as he hears me approaching. He is dressed simply, but formally. A white button down shirt is tucked into simple black dress pants, and black oxfords laced carefully peek out from the hem. His hair has been neatly combed, unusual for him. Once I walk closer to him, I notice that he smells of lemon soap and shaving cream.

'You clean up well,' I tell him.

He scoffs, holding back a laugh. 'So do you. I don't think I have seen you in a dress and heels since...' he trails off, realising what he was about to say.

He didn't mean to bring it up, but I knew what he was

referring to; my father's funeral and how I had refused to attend in the end and how my father couldn't be here today when I graduate. Harvey coughs to break the silence and then gestures with his right hand as a signal for us to start walking.

We walk back down the hall and through the foyer, and then back down another hall until we reach the cafeteria. It is a spacious room, easily fitting twelve tables, with chairs tucked neatly under them. The walls are white, while the floor is a faux-marble linoleum. I head towards the self-serving station at the back of the room and grab trays for both of us, handing one to Harvey. The community centre is open twenty-four/seven, and always serves food in the cafeteria, though the aristocrats never eat here. I survey the food. This is a pointless act as I pick out the same thing as I always do: scrambled eggs, bacon, and fresh fruit. I pile these onto my tray, as well as a bottle of water, and then head over to our table in the far corner.

I sit down and wait for Harvey; he always takes longer because of the sheer amount of food he picks out. When he does sit down next to me, he begins scarfing down his food immediately, barely taking a breath between each mouthful. I shake my head at him as I look down at my food and slowly began eating my eggs. They always taste like they have been sitting for too long in the bain-marie. After several mouthfuls, I eventually abandon eating my eggs and pick up a piece of bacon to nibble on. Harvey is still deep into his food and won't be coming up for air anytime soon.

When we are done with breakfast, we walk our trays over and scrape our leftovers into the bin before leaving our trays to be collected and walk back out of the cafeteria.

We walk back through the community centre until we reach the outside. The sun is fully up now, bathing the city in its warmth and light. I look over to Harvey, who nods for me to continue leading the way back over to the town hall. We walk in silence, both of us deep in thought about this morning's events.

When we reach town hall, others from our graduating year have already arrived and are waiting outside in the quad for the doors to the town hall to open. I can see kids I went to school with standing awkwardly with their parents, and I wonder how many of this year's graduates have actually applied for jobs or further education. *Not many.*

I search around until I come across my mother standing over near the fountain with Harvey's father, and we head towards them. My mum is tall and lean with dirty blonde hair that is always pulled back into a neat bun on top her head. Her rounded face is full of old laugh lines around her lips that never smile, and her eyes are of the same olive green as mine. Today, she wears a black pencil skirt to her knees, complemented by a simple white short-sleeved blouse and black peep-toes that, unsurprisingly, are the same as the ones she had bought for me.

Harvey's father, Edward, stands next to my mother and they are chatting absently, probably about how this morning would pan out. Edward is tall and muscular, with close-cropped dark brown hair and the same jaw line as his son's. The only real significant difference between their faces is that Edward always had dark circles under his eyes, a sign that he worked too much. He is the captain of the Guard, but today, he is dressed in a more formal attire than his captain's uniform.

'Luka, you look so lovely,' my mother praises, 'and Harvey, you clean up so nicely.' She beams.

'Thank you,' Harvey replies for both of us.

'Yes, Luka, you really do look lovely. It's not often we see you so dressed up,' Edward comments lightly.

I reply with a faint smile.

'Well,' my mother says, 'it looks like they've finally opened the doors. Let's head inside and find our seats.' With that decided, we all proceed to the town hall, following countless other families as we ascend the steps and walk inside the doorway to our future.

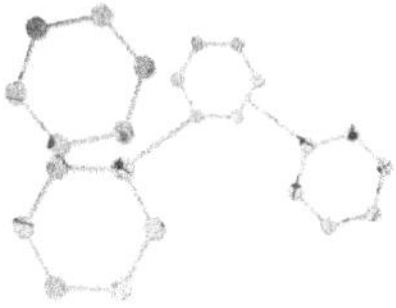

TWO

THE TOWN HALL is immaculate on the inside. The foyer has a ten-foot-high ceiling with white walls and polished marble floors. The reception area is at the back of the foyer. It is made up of a white desk that runs the length of the room with six translucent computer screens visible above it, and a person behind each screen. The reception assists with inquiries, paperwork, complaints, and anything else that needs to be addressed by the council or the senate.

We follow the flow of people down the west wing, which is a large hallway with several doors branching off of it, probably offices for council and senate officials. We come to the end of the hallway and reach a set of double doors that have been propped open to allow easy entry into the amphitheatre.

The amphitheatre is a vast, circular room that holds extensive rows and columns of seats that cascade down until it reaches a large stage at the bottom. The seats are separated by aisles, and we walk down the nearest one, find the first available four seats, and sit down. Other families have similar ideas and take their seats at the first available seats they can find, though some insist on finding the best view of the stage before sitting down.

The stage at the bottom of the amphitheatre is made of

wood, and warm golden light shines down on it from the bulbs above. Towards the front of the stage is a podium, a slim glass structure that stands about a metre from the stage floor topped with a microphone and small camera. Today's ceremony will be televised live across the nation.

A woman with tight black curls and a weathered face walks onto the stage. She wears an elegant navy blue pantsuit. She reaches the podium and calls everyone to attention.

'Good morning, everyone, I am Vivian Melbrook, and I would like to welcome you all here on this special occasion. Today, this year's graduates will receive their acceptance letters in their chosen fields.' She pauses just long enough for that to sink in.

'Now, before we begin, I could like to welcome our Chancellor to the stage to say a few kind words to this year's graduates.' There is a polite applause as Vivian exits the stage and Chancellor Cain walks on.

The chancellor is our country's selected leader. Each city has a small council that reports directly to the senate, which is the council for the Capital city, my city. The chancellor is elected by the senate to become our leader. Chancellor Cain is the only chancellor I have ever known. My father used to tell me stories about him. He said that Cain was elected to power at a young age, and is the only chancellor to be re-elected by the senate after his term of ten years, allowing him to rule for a second term. This year is Cain's nineteenth year as chancellor. After his term is up in another year, he will not be re-elected, as is our law. I am curious to see who the senate will elect as our new chancellor.

Cain is a tall man with a slim build, round face and sandy blonde hair, with specks of grey. Cain has reached the podium, and he stops to clear his throat first before speaking.

'Good morning, citizens,' he says, with a husky voice. 'I

would like to welcome all of those here today who will be receiving their acceptance letters, and their families that have come to witness this significant occasion.

'Graduates, you have all successfully completed your schooling and have applied for your field of choice, whether that be as further education and training or full-fledged employment.' He pauses, assessing the crowd.

'You have all worked exceptionally hard and I am sure you have been waiting in anticipation over this last month to find out whether you have been accepted into your first, second or third field of choice. It goes without saying that no matter what field you end up in, and no matter what preference of choice, I know that each and every one of you will become a valuable member of our society.

'I look forward to meeting the new recruits who will be joining the enlistment for our Delta Force and our scientific division—I know that each and every one of you chosen will do your very best to help our country in this war against the remaining Genesi. I look forward to working alongside all of you. Best of luck to you all.'

I applaud politely as the crowd around me cheers at the conclusion of his speech. After a brief silence, Vivian walks back on stage, carrying a large box and stands beside Cain.

Cain clears his throat once more before calling out the first name. 'Garry Anderson,' he calls into the microphone.

Garry stands from his place in the crowd and begins his way to the stage. He is thin, and the size of his glasses makes him seem even smaller. He is dressed formally, as are we all. He steps onto the stage and walks over to Cain who shakes his hand and congratulates him. Vivian hands the boy his acceptance letter from the box she is holding. He thanks them both and continues off the other side of the stage heading back to his seat.

'Rebecca Attwood,' Cain calls into the microphone. A young girl with short brown hair stands up and makes her way towards the stage. She is dressed in a deep red dress that falls just below her knees. She makes her way onto the stage where she too shakes hands with the chancellor and is handed her acceptance letter.

The list continues and I can't help but tune out and go over my plans once more in my head. I am pulled out of my reverie by Harvey's nudging elbow. I look over to him and realise my name has been called. I stand and smooth the wrinkles in my dress. In my unease, I notice my palms are sweating slightly; I quickly wipe them on my dress. I shuffle past Harvey and exit the row of seats. I take careful strides down the aisle, noticing that I can feel my heart racing.

As I make it to the steps leading to the stage, I can't help but notice that the stage is actually made of marble not wood. It just looks like wood. I keep my head down until I am just a few feet away from the chancellor. I look up and met his gaze. Up close, he looks much older than what I expected. His hair is definitely more grey than blonde. He has crow's feet around his black eyes and fine wrinkles around his face.

He smiles at me as I approach. 'Congratulations, Miss Foster, your father would be so proud of you.'

I continue to hold his gaze, 'Thank you, Chancellor Cain,' I say, relieved that my voice does not give away how nervous I feel in his presence. *Why do I feel so nervous?*

As Vivian hands me my letter, the chancellor continues to speak. 'I look forward to getting to know you better and seeing first-hand what you can accomplish. Here's hoping that you are your father's daughter, I would love to see a mind like yours deployed into the field. Let's just hope that if that happens, you don't meet the same fate as my son.' He is smiling, but his expression is serious.

Cain's son, Sam, was deployed immediately after he graduated from Delta Force training. The entire event was televised and everyone cheered for the chancellor's son. Only two members of his unit returned and he was not one of them. All but two of them killed by the Genesi. I hope Harvey and I do not meet the same fate.

'Thank you, sir,' I say, before walking away and descending offstage.

I return to my seat and my mum gives me a knowing look, almost as if she had heard what the chancellor had said to me. I sit down in my seat and look over at Harvey.

'What did he say?' he whispers in my ear.

I lean in closer to him and keep my voice a low whisper. 'He said he looks forward to getting to know me better and seeing what I can accomplish.'

'Does that mean you got in? Is that what he was trying to tell you?' he says, voice rising in excitement.

'Shush. I don't know; I feel like it has a deeper meaning than that. He creeped me out, actually.' Harvey gives me a quizzical look, but remains silent, knowing he will have to wait until we are alone to ask me. We both sit in silence until Harvey's name is called.

I watch as he makes his way down the aisle and onto the stage. He keeps his head down until he reaches the chancellor. Chancellor Cain congratulates him and I watch Harvey thank him as they shake hands before he receives his letter from Vivian. Before I know it, he is sitting back down in his seat next to mine and I can finally breathe again.

The list of names continues and I tune out again. Why had Cain said what he said? And why only to me? I hadn't noticed him say anything more than 'Congratulations' to anyone else. *Why only me? Did he suspect something about me? What did his message mean?*

After what felt like hours, and it probably was, Chancellor Cain addressed the audience once more. 'Congratulations to each and every one of you, and I would like to use this medium to thank all the families and loved ones present here today to witness this momentous occasion, as this year's graduates become adults and fully-fledged members of our society. Tomorrow is a new day, one where you will all begin the next chapters of your lives. Thank you. And long live these United Nations.'

'Long live these United Nations,' the crowd murmurs.

We all stand to make our way out of the amphitheatre, but we have to wait our turn as others make their way into the aisle and through the doors. When it is our turn, we head back to the foyer in silence. It is not until we have walked back out into the quad that any of us dare speak.

Harvey's dad and my mum carpooled to get here, so Harvey and I follow Edward as he leads the way from the quad to the private car park behind it. Being Captain of the Guard does have its perks; everyone else would have to walk at least a block before they reach the nearest car park.

Edward's car is a shiny black sedan—standard-issue given to all members of the city's police force. Once we're seated—Harvey and I in the back, and Mum in the passenger seat, Edward turns the ignition. The car purrs to life and we begin our journey home. The drive through the city will take us ten minutes, compared to the hour-long jog it took Harvey and I this morning.

We reach the gate. Sam is still on-duty. 'Captain Montgomery, nice to see you again this morning, Sir.'

'And you, Deputy Hale,' Edward replies kindly. I watch as Sam inspects the car and assesses us all before turning to open the gates and waving us through. Eventually we reach the Montgomerys family's house. They, too, have a long drive that leads to a house that is identical to ours.

Harvey's house looks incredibly different to ours on the inside, though. I thought that it was probably because it lacked a woman's touch, which is what you would expect from a widowed father. The house is sparsely furnished with no memorabilia. I turn to the right and walk towards the living room. The room has a high ceiling with a plush black leather lounge that sits in front of the room's fireplace. A few bookshelves line the walls, but other than that, the room is quite bare. We all stand around, none of us knowing what to do or who should go first.

'Why don't we all sit down?' As always, my mother is the one to break the silence. After a quick moment, I take a seat in the middle of the lounge, Harvey sits down right next to me, mum takes the spot to my left, and Edward sits next to Harvey.

Another moment of silence. None of us knowing what to say; we are all dreading opening the letters.

'I guess I'll go first,' Harvey finally speaks. 'That way, if it is bad news, we know yours will at least be good news.'

Dread fills the pit of my stomach. *What if he doesn't get in, what will we do?*

Harvey carefully tears open the envelope and pulls out the letter with trepidation. He unfolds the paper, letting his eyes scan it before he reads it out loud to the rest of us.

'Dear Mr Montgomery, the senate and its Military have taken the valuable time to review and assess your application along with your aptitude test results. It is with great pleasure that we inform you that you have been accepted as one of the successful candidates to be considered for Delta Force.' He stops reading and I let a breath escape that I hadn't realised I had been holding. *Harvey got in.*

I lean over his shoulder to read the rest of the letter, only stopping when I have read it in full.

'It says you fly out at 06:00 hours tomorrow.'

Edward gives a resigned look; he would be saying good-bye to his son tomorrow and the only family he has left. He notices me looking at him and gives a small, sad smile.

'Why don't you open your letter, Luka, and we will see what it says,' he says to me.

I nod and turn my attention to the envelope sitting in my lap. This is it; this small envelope is what holds the outcome of my future and all of my plans. I clench and unclench my fingers a few times to stop them from shaking. Carefully, I open the envelope, taking my time to gather my thoughts and calm the storm that is raging in my stomach. I slide the letter from the envelope and carefully unfold it. My eyes scan the first paragraph.

'I got in; I ship out at 06:00 hours with Harvey tomorrow.' I sigh with relief.

I am one of the five percent of females considered for Delta Force. I look over at Harvey and he gives me a half smile. At least we have each other, no matter what comes at us, we will face it *together*.

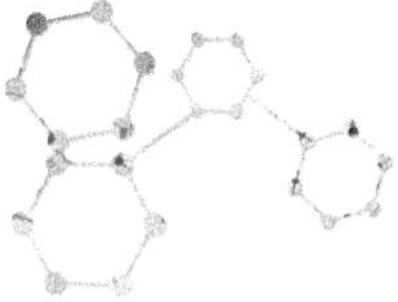

THREE

I AM STANDING inside my father's office, something I have not done in almost ten years. The bookshelves and books have been placed back to their rightful places, the desk has been turned right side up and a new computer sits in the place where the destroyed one once sat, but still I have not returned to this room since that day.

I run my fingers along the bookshelves as I make my way slowly over to the desk and sit down in the chair that my father had once sat in for all those years. Unshed tears fill my vision as I gaze at the old family photo that lives next to the computer. The photo was taken only a few months before my father's death. We look so happy; I had a big smile on my face as I sat in between my parents to take the photo. They were trying not to laugh at how excited I was at being allowed to take a family photo myself. We all looked so young and innocent, completely unaware and unprepared that our lives would never see such joy again. My throat burns from holding back the tears.

I stand up and take one final look around the office, committing the image of it to memory and walk towards the door, shutting it firmly behind me. My mother is waiting for me in the entry and I walk down the hallway towards her.

She looks tired; her eyes are red-rimmed from staying up most of the night crying. She doesn't have to say, but I know that she is thinking of my father, about how she must be feeling like she is losing us both. She puts on a brave face as she smiles at my approach, but I see the sadness in her eyes, I see how hard this is for her.

'Are you ready?' she asks me, her voice wavering only slightly.

'Yes, I have everything I need,' I answer, and then stop to hug her. I fold my arms around the small of her back, gripping tightly. She holds me too. I breathe in the scent of her shampoo; it smells of coconut and spearmint; I commit that to memory. After a moment, I pull away from her, bending down to pick up my duffle bag and walk out the front door for the last time.

The car is parked in the drive at the front of the house. It is the colour of liquid silver. I open the back door and throw my duffle bag on the seat before climbing into the front passenger seat and clipping my seatbelt. Mum hops into the driver's side and starts the engine. We drive to the airport in silence, both of us at a loss for words.

When we arrive, I grab my duffle bag and get out of the car. Mum locks the car and we head inside. I'm immediately greeted with a blast of frigid air. The foyer is spacious and void of colour. White walls, ceiling and, floor—there isn't much else here aside from a front desk—also white. The lady behind the desk is easy to spot, her chocolate skin and deep ebony hair are a stark contrast to the crisp white around her. I bypass her, though, turning to the left towards the waiting area that leads to the hangar.

I see Harvey and his dad saying their goodbyes. I turn to my mother; she looks up at me with tear-filled eyes. Guilt stabs at my heart.

'I am going to miss you so, so much. You know that, right?' she says, her voice breaking.

'I know, I'm going to miss you too,' I reply honestly.

She wipes a tear from her face. 'I am so proud of you, and I know your father would be proud of you too and the woman you are becoming.' I smile in reply. 'Now, I don't want you to think of me once you leave,' she continues. 'I don't want you to be held back by thoughts of your father or me; I want you to walk out that door and never look back. Do you understand?'

She looks me directly in the eyes and I hesitate.

'I can't do that, Mum,' I say finally, my voice thick.

'Yes, you can and you *must*, you will forget about us and live your life with purpose, you can't be held back by regret because it may get you killed.' Her tears began running in earnest, sliding down her face, pooling on her chin before dripping off onto the floor.

She hugs me one last time, a tight squeeze. We stay like that for several moments until reluctantly she lets me go, her eyes spilling over as she takes in my features one last time, committing them to memory.

'I love you,' she says.

'I love you too, Mum, and I will *never* forget you.'

She drops her hands from my face and ushers for me to go. I turn and walk away from her for what could be the last time I will ever see her. A hollow ache fills my chest.

I stop to say goodbye to Edward as I head towards the hangar door where Harvey waits. I tell him that Harvey and I will take good care of one another and he gives me a quick hug. I take one final look back at my mum as I walk through the door, holding back the tears that threaten to fill my eyes.

We walk into the hangar in silence. The other recruits are already waiting to board. There are seven of us in total and I am the only female. A few smile at Harvey as we walk over to stand and wait, I recognise them from school.

One boy I'm more familiar with is Lewis Kingston. He is tall and lean with somewhat pale skin and a round face. He has shaggy, dark blonde hair and, from what I remember from school, he was quite intelligent, with a particular talent for computers. *That must be why they want him in Delta Force.*

A female officer holding a clipboard approaches us. 'Name?' she barks at me, her voice ringing with authority. The tightness of her ponytail pulls at the skin around her face, giving her a severe countenance.

'Luka Foster,' I state. She scribbles on her clipboard without looking up. She then turns her attention to Harvey.

'Name?'

'Harvey Montgomery.'

She marks his names off the checklist and strides toward the hovercraft. When she reaches it, she stops suddenly and turns to face us all. I notice that her tanned skin is unmarred by makeup of any kind.

She addresses the group, her voice loud and clear. 'Now that you are all here, my name is Lieutenant Yates. You may board the craft. Please, place your bags overhead and secure them carefully before taking your seat. Once you are seated, I will run through instructions on how to buckle yourself in correctly and the pre-flight safety instructions.'

One by one we form a line and walk up the small ramp that leads inside the hovercraft.

Inside the craft, there are ten seats mounted on each of the long, metal walls. Each seat has its own safety harness and overhead compartment. The first thing I notice is that there are no windows. The only view outside the craft is through the cockpit and out the hovercraft's windscreen. I can see inside the cockpit now; the pilot wears a white helmet, so I can't make out his face.

I pick the seat closest to me and store my duffle bag in the overhead compartment, using the buckles and straps to hold it in place. Harvey does the same at the seat beside me. Bags successfully stowed, Harvey and I take our seats, waiting for further instructions. I glance around me as everyone stores their bags and take their seats; Lewis takes the seat next to Harvey.

When everyone has taken their seats on the craft, Lieutenant Yates moves to stand in the middle of the aisle so that she can be seen clearly.

'Now that you are all seated, I will show you how to buckle yourself in correctly. There are four straps in total, but only one that holds the buckle. You need to clip the remaining three straps into the buckle, ensuring that they are placed over your shoulders and legs with the buckle resting in the middle of your chest. You will need to ensure that the harness is secured tightly to your bodice.'

She sits down in the nearest seat and begins buckling herself in as a demonstration. I watch carefully. Once her demonstration is complete, she nods for us to strap ourselves in.

I find that after buckling myself in, the straps are still loose on me, so I tighten them slightly until I am sure they are tight enough to keep me in place.

'We will begin our journey to the training facility in a few minutes,' Lieutenant Yates explains once we're all strapped in. 'You must not unbuckle your belt or leave your seat under *any* circumstances,' she says sternly. 'It will take us approximately four hours to reach the facility. You may feel your ears pop once we are up in the air, that is perfectly normal and the sensation should stop once we have reached the right altitude. There are no bathrooms on this craft, so you will need to hold on until we arrive at the training facility. If you wish to talk among yourselves, please do so quietly.'

The hovercraft powers up, making a quiet humming noise. I can feel the vibrations of the craft right down to my bones. I look beside me at Harvey. I can tell he is just as nervous as I am. Neither of us has been on a hovercraft before.

Hovercrafts are only used to transport a person between the cities if your job requires it. Only those in the military, senate or council ever get to leave the safety of the city walls. The only occasion for a civilian to use a hovercraft is if their occupation is needed in another city. Otherwise, civilians never see the outside of the wall. We only know what is outside the walls thanks to the history books and videos at school when we are taught about the war and of the Genesi. Only the chancellor, the senate and the Delta Force know what lies outside the walls.

The hovercraft slowly begins to rise, causing a strange sensation to go through my body, almost like vertigo. My heartbeat begins to race and I can feel my pulse involuntarily quickening, beating in my ears.

It continues to rise into the air slowly, and just like the officer had warned us, both of my ears pop, causing an uncomfortable feeling in my ears and muffling my hearing. Thankfully, it only lasts a few seconds before my hearing returns to normal and my heart rate begins to slow.

At least my anxiety did not take over. I would have to do my best to remain calm and keep my heart rate steady for the next four hours. I have kept my anxiety hidden, knowing that if I were found out, I would not have been accepted. Not even Harvey knows, as my attacks don't usually happen around him.

Harvey is bouncing his right leg up and down nervously. I reach over and place my hand on his knee, pushing down slightly to make the bouncing stop. He looks over at me sheepishly.

'It's fine; I'm nervous too,' I reassure him.

We sit in silence for most of the journey. There is hardly any conversation, as everyone on board is too nervous to break the silence. The hum of the hovercraft is the only noise around us. After almost four hours, the officer announces that we will be landing in ten minutes' time.

There are murmurs through the craft. What the training facility would be like? Would it be inside a wall too just like the cities? Will we get to eat when we get there? Will we meet the general? Will we meet the chancellor again? All of this I tune out, having spent enough time thinking about this prior to leaving.

As we begin our decent, I am met with the uncomfortable feeling of my ears popping again, readjusting to the decline in altitude. The hovercraft lightly touches down, and the sounds of seatbelts being unbuckled echoes throughout the craft.

I unclip my harness and move the straps out of my way as I stand, my legs wobbling. I reach to unstrap my duffle bag from the overhead compartment and sling it over my shoulder before turning around and awaiting further instructions.

Lieutenant Yates motions for us to follow her out of the hovercraft. We file out of the craft and make our way down the ramp before stepping down onto the asphalt.

We are standing in a much larger version of the airport's hanger from back home. I can see several other hovercrafts parked along the hanger as we make our way out and into the airport building. I see no other recruits or soldiers in the hanger.

We enter the airport and pass through the waiting area to the foyer. It is almost a replica of the one back home, aside from the fact that it is twice the size and there is nobody seated at the front desk. Instead of one set of doors leading from the airport, there are three.

We follow Lieutenant Yates out of the airport doors that are to the far left and into a large hallway that connects their airport to another building. Its walls and floor are the same as the inside of the airports foyer, all white. We follow down the long hallway.

When we reach a set of double doors, Lieutenant Yates stops and pulls out a security access card from a pocket and swipes it into a small slot on the wall next to the doors, which then slide open with a slight whooshing sound. We all follow through the doors and into an identical hallway. I suspect that this facility is designed purposely so that it is near impossible to map out. *Near* impossible, but not entirely impossible.

She leads us down the hallway, taking a left turn before we reach a door at the end of the hall. She stops to swipe open another door, which slides open to revel a stairwell.

Lieutenant Yates leads us down two flights of stairs, taking us two levels underground before she again swipes her card to open a door, leading us out of the stairwell. We walk out of the stairwell and into another identical hallway. I am careful to commit all of this to memory. You can never be certain of what information could come in handy one day.

We turn left and are led down the hallway. After some distance, we begin to pass doors on either side of us. She leads us to the tenth door, right at the left-hand end of the hallway and swipes her access card to open the door. She gestures for us to enter and we follow her single file into the room.

Single beds line the walls, five on either side, making ten in total. There are two doors at the back of the room; one read male, the other female. Bathrooms.

'This is dormitory Alpha,' announces Lieutenant Yates. 'I will read the names of those staying in this dormitory for the duration of their training; the remaining beds will be filled with other recruits from other cities as they arrive. There are ten dormitories in total. The other doors along the hall are the other dormitories. You are not permitted to enter a dormitory that is not your own.

'Bathrooms are at the back. Within, you will find toilets, basins and showers in there. I will leave you to pick your beds and get settled as you wait for the remaining recruits to arrive.

'Lewis Kingston, Harvey Montgomery and Luka Foster,' she says, directing her attention towards us. 'You three will be in this dormitory.' She turns away, 'The rest of you should follow me and I will show you to your dormitories.'

She pivots on her heel and leaves Harvey, Lewis and me standing in silence as the others follow her out.

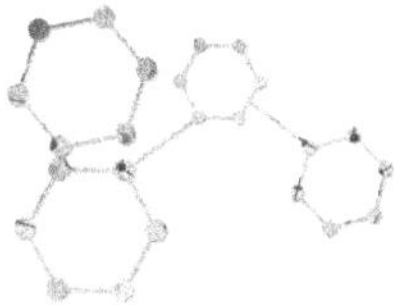

FOUR

AT FIRST, NO one moved, then, as if someone had flipped a switch, we all turn to face the beds.

I pick the bed closest to the door, while Harvey chooses the bed next to mine.

The third bed down was claimed by Lewis, who threw his bag down and then headed towards the back of the dorm where the bathrooms were located. Harvey plopped down onto his bunk, stretching out and putting his hands behind his head.

'We better get comfortable, I get the feeling it will be awhile before anyone else arrives and then even longer again before we are allowed to leave this dorm,' he says.

I turn and sit down on my bed, my legs dangling over the side. The mattress is harder than I expect it to be. The luxuries I am used to are beginning to feel like a distant memory.

'What do you suppose the rest of the facility looks like?' I ask once I am finally comfortable.

'Not sure. She made a point of not telling us anything when we arrived,' he says, and I nod, having noticed the same thing. 'I'm guessing they don't want us knowing our way around the facility, or maybe we will be given a tour of the place once we are all together,' he continues.

I scoff. 'I doubt it, given the security in this place. I bet we won't be shown around and we won't get access to any parts of the facility other than our dorms, the training rooms, and the mess hall.'

Harvey scratches his chin, absorbing this. 'Probably,' he says slowly. 'Although the secrecy does make me question what they could be trying to hide in a place like this; it is just a training facility.' He looks around him briefly before turning back to me. 'Not that it would stop you from trying to find out. I am sure you can find a way to bypass the security in this place.' He knows me well.

'I wonder if the security in this place is for our protection, or for theirs,' I say. 'My father used to come to this city when I was younger, to visit the main base and the general. He said that the security was always tight, but that if you were smart enough, you could easily find a way around the security.'

'I think he meant if *you* specifically were smart enough, not just anybody. Do you think that your father came here because of the classified project the chancellor had him working on?'

'I think so, which would mean that the general was probably a part of it too and that Chancellor Cain was not working alone.'

'Do you think that anyone else might have known about it, anyone in the senate maybe?'

'I am not sure, the video my father left for me to find cuts out after a few minutes. I wish I'd got to find out what he was trying to warn me about.'

Harvey nods, agreeing.

Breaking our silence is the bathroom door opening, as Lewis walks back into the room.

'Hey guys,' he says with an awkward wave of his hand. 'Looks like we have a bit of time to kill.' He walks over and sits down on his bunk. 'What made you two want to enlist?' he asks us, his face expectant.

The truth is too much to share with a relative stranger. So, I use my practiced lie.

'Well, I guess my reason is obvious, I want to be the first female to make it into Delta Force. I want to be the first female deployed outside the walls.'

'And I'm here to make sure she doesn't get herself killed,' Harvey jokes. He and I both know I can take care of myself.

When I asked Harvey's father a few years ago why it was that no female had ever been sent out into the field, he told me it was because female soldiers were rare. That the senate and the military both felt that a female soldier was not as expendable as a male soldier because females are heavily relied upon to ensure the survival of the human race. Edward said that that was the reason only five out of a hundred candidates were recruited. He also told me that of the few females who have made it into the Delta Force unit, they were never sent into the field. They were stationed on base to oversee that the Delta Force unit's missions went smoothly. I needed to ensure that did not happen to me.

I *had* to make sure that I made it outside the walls.

'Wow, you two must really love each other if you are willing to enlist together.'

I choke back a laugh.

Harvey coughs and rubs his neck, something he does when he is uncomfortable. His cheeks are flushed scarlet.

'We do, but not like that,' I look over at him, hoping I haven't made him feel worse.

'We made a promise to each other when we were younger that we would always look out for each other.' He pauses before continuing. 'I'm here to keep that promise, but also because I want to observe them, the Genesi, see if they really are as savage as history tells us they are or if maybe they have evolved since then. For all we know, the Genesi coding could have been diluted and bred out of their genetics over the last century.'

'I've always wondered that too' Lewis replies. I frown inwardly. So much for not telling him the truth.

'What made you want to join, Lewis?' I ask, changing the subject.

'Um... well,' he reaches up and rubs the back of his neck with his right hand. 'My mum raised me and my three younger siblings by herself. I'm the oldest, the other three are all still under twelve. It's been tough on my mum, providing for us all. I wanted to help.' He shrugs, looking down at the floor, waiting for us to judge him for his background.

Harvey speaks up. 'Wanting to help your family is a pure motive.'

Lewis gives an awkward half smile. 'Thanks, though I am not sure others will see it that way. I think it's only a matter of time before I get labelled as the "poor kid",' he says with a wry smile. I felt bad for him; it sounds like he's had a hard life. I could sympathise. I knew only too well what that's like.

'Harvey and I have got your back,' I tell him honestly. Lewis smiles. For the first time since my father died, I feel as if it might be possible to get close to someone other than Harvey. Harvey smiles at me reassuringly, and I know that he is proud of me for trying.

* * *

HARVEY, LEWIS AND I spend some time absently chatting about what to expect from our training. After some time, we are interrupted as the door clicks open. We jump to our feet to stand at attention as a male officer enters the room.

He is dressed in army regulation uniform: black cargo pants, short sleeve button-up cargo shirt, and black boots with laces double knotted. He has close-cropped red hair and his face is covered in freckles. As he enters the room, he is followed by seven others. Recruits.

The first recruit into the room is tall and broad-shouldered with a stocky, muscular build. He looks to be the same age as Lewis, Harvey and I: around about eighteen. He has dark brown hair that looks closer to black because it is so shortly cropped. He has high cheekbones and thin lips that are pressed tightly together, though there are crease lines around his eyes, telling me he squints when he concentrates. His lips curve arrogantly, and he turns his eyes to Harvey, then Lewis, and finally to me. I suppress a shudder. I can tell he is sizing me up, assessing if I am worth considering as a threat before eventually disregarding me as he takes in the remainder of the dorm. He is smart; I saw the intelligence in his eyes as he looked at me. His expression doesn't give his intelligence away, though, it is hidden under his mask of arrogance. He clearly doesn't want people knowing what he can do. All of this tells me that he is not a leader, but favours self-preservation. I get the distinct feeling that this recruit could threaten my plans. It is best that I do not become a threat to him.

Behind the dark-haired guy, is a female recruit, which surprises me. She is tall and lean, with the skin colour of deep caramel. Her hair so dark brown that it looks like dark chocolate and it hangs in loose waves down her back. She has high cheekbones and full, plump lips. She is stunningly beautiful except for her expression, which is hard and ruthless. She looks me up and down, the same as the previous recruit, assessing me. I assume that she expected to be the only female in this room and is none too pleased when her eyes take me in. The way her eyes flick to the first recruit suggest she has underlying feelings for him. Likely, she joined Delta Force because of him. Not a likely ally.

The next two recruits are identical twins of the same age as the rest of us. They have deep brown skin and are incredibly tall; their bodies ripple with muscles and strength. They both have full lips and shortly cropped dark brown, almost black hair. It will be difficult telling these two apart; I would have to assess their personalities to be able to tell one from the other. I'd be willing to bet that they have never spent a day apart. The logical thing to do would have been to separate them into different dormitories in order to determine their full individual potential. Undetermined ally.

A boy with curly chestnut hair and pale skin enters the room after the twins. He is tall with broad shoulders, and I can see the muscles in his shoulders working as he walks into the room. He is followed by an Asian boy with pale skin and black, straight hair that is long enough to fall into his eyes. The Asian boy is wiry, and looks like he would be an excellent runner. My attention is drawn from him to the last recruit that walks into the room.

The final recruit is tall, and the lean muscles of his body are clearly visible beneath his clothes. He has black hair that has grown past his ears and is beginning to curl at the ends. He has full, pink lips with long dark eyelashes and a heart-shaped face with a strong jaw. Unlike the others, he pays no attention to his surroundings and does not lift his gaze from the floor in front of him. I am guessing that most people assume he's shy, but I had a feeling it was more than that. I felt like he didn't want to be here.

As if he felt my gaze, he looks up to meet my eyes from across the room. Unlike the others, he does not look surprised to see me standing there. We seem to stare at each other, but I can't read him. He clearly is guarding his thoughts. I figured there was either nothing significant about him, or he is doing a tremendous job at keeping people like me from being able to read him. I am instantly drawn to him.

My attention is pulled away as the officer clears his throat.

'This is dormitory Alpha. You will be staying in this dormitory for the entire duration of your training. The three recruits you see in front of you will also be staying in this dormitory. From now on, you will be referred to as Alpha unit. I suggest you make yourselves acquainted.

'The bathrooms are at the back; you will find toilets, basins and showers in there. Males are not permitted to use or enter the female bathrooms and vice versa. I will leave you to pick your beds and get acquainted with one another; I will return at noon to lead you to the mess hall for lunch.'

'After lunch, all recruits will be introduced to General Thorn and Chancellor Cain.' With the conclusion of his speech, he turns on his heel and marches out of the dormitory, letting the door close behind him and leaving us all in uncomfortable silence.

One by one, they all begin to claim their beds. Naturally, the girl chooses the bed beside the first boy. The mysterious boy was the only person to have not claimed a bed yet. With a small, silent sigh, he strides over, and with more care than I expect, gently places his duffle bag on the spare bunk beside Lewis and sits down next to his bag.

The first recruit strides towards us, stopping directly in front of Harvey and me, folding his arms across his chest. *Great, here we go.*

'So, I believe introductions are in order, who do we have here?' he asks with a smirk, his voice higher than I had expected it to be and laced with arrogance. Harvey just stares at the boy, his face an unreadable mask to anyone except me, but I can tell that the boy has annoyed him.

'Seeing as we were here first, how about you tell us who *you* are,' I say, rising to my feet, and drawing his attention away from Harvey and back to myself. The boy looks at me sharply and, comes to stand directly in front of me. The entire room is watching us, the air filled with tension. Exactly what I was supposed to avoid.

He laughs in my face, but it sounds false. 'You don't scare me, little girl,' he spits.

I supress the laugh threatening to bubble out of me. 'And your pathetic attempt to dominate us through fear does not scare me,' I hold his gaze; I cannot back down now, otherwise, he will think he has won.

He chuckles at my words, 'I'd watch myself if I were you, *princess*. You're dangerously close to making enemies before training has even begun.'

A threat. I smile at him, antagonising him further. 'I can take care of myself.' Smugness radiates off of him as we glare at each other, then something else flashes across his face and is hidden in an instant. *Recognition.*

'Oh my God, Ian. This is stupid! *I'll* introduce everybody if you two would just get over yourselves,' says the girl. 'I'm Skai Mendez,' she gestures towards the boy in front of me, 'That's Ian Jenson,' at the mention of his name, the first recruit, Ian, steps back from me to shoot the girl, Skai, a pained look that she pointedly ignores as she continues introducing everybody in the room, her voice full of confidence.

She points towards the twins. 'This is Taylor and Tyler Jackson—*don't* ask me which one is which; I can never tell,' she says, rolling her eyes. 'This kid is Beau Carter,' she points towards the boy with the chestnut hair, 'and that's Emory Nuggen, or however the hell you pronounce it.'

'Nguyen,' Emory chimes in before quickly closing his mouth, as if he were afraid of her.

'*Whatever*; now that you know all of our names, how about you tell us yours.'

I'd love to slap the attitude from her face.

I notice that she left the name of the last recruit; I suppose it is possible that he did not arrive with them.

Lewis breaks the awkward silence. 'I'm Lewis Kingston,' he says with a small, awkward wave of his hand.

'Harvey Montgomery,' I hear Harvey say.

I sigh. 'Luka Foster.'

Ian smirks and I clamp my jaw shut to avoid punching him in the face, 'Foster eh? Does that make you the daughter of Christopher Foster, that scientist who died, you know?'

I raise an eyebrow, challenging. *You and I both know that you know exactly who I am.*

There would be no escaping the association with my father and his murder. Everybody had heard about my father's murder, broadcast as it was across every city.

'So what if she is—what's it to you?' Harvey, always coming to my aid.

'Well then, I guess that explains why a weak little girl like you got accepted into the Delta Force training, wouldn't you say, guys?' He asks the room. No one answers.

A cruel stab. I expected comments like this to be made, but it still hurt nonetheless. I was more than just my name. Not that I blame anyone for thinking that, my family were entitled to penance after my father's death because of his importance, and being female, my abilities would be second-guessed here.

'It doesn't matter who her father is, she got accepted on her own merit just like everyone else in this room,' Harvey went on. Ian had clearly pissed him off.

'Yeah, I am sure that's it,' he says sarcastically, eyes rolling.

Calm down, Luka, you cannot hit a recruit on your first day. Instead, I put my hand on Harvey's chest, pushing him away from Ian and step between the two boys.

'Look, guys, whatever our reasons for being here, we all have to live together, so let's just try to get along,' says Lewis, trying for the role of mediator and failing. He immediately regrets his words as Ian's attention is now brought to him as he makes his way across the room towards Lewis. Lewis takes a step back, but is blocked by Skai.

I tense, ready to jump in if he tries anything on Lewis, but Ian is stopped halfway as the mystery boy stands in the way, blocking Ian from reaching Lewis.

'And who the *hell* are you?' Ian demands.

'I thought he came with you guys,' Harvey says.

'As if trash like that would be from our city,' Skai mutters, loud enough for the room to hear.

Ian turns back to face the boy and asks with deliberate slowness, 'Who. *The hell.* Are you?' All eyes are on the mysterious boy, waiting for him to speak.

'Ren Mason,' he grinds out, his voice husky.

Everyone looks as puzzled.

'What city are you from?' Ian is clearly not going to let the subject drop.

'Not really any of your business,' Ren says casually, while walking back towards his bunk and sitting down again.

'None of my business,' Ian repeats clearly annoyed. 'Of course, it's my business if I have to sleep in a room for the next six months with some *psycho*. What city are you from?'

he demands. His fists are clenched at his sides.

Ren ignores him, clearly done talking, which causes a vein to bulge in Ian's neck.

'Well, *Ren Mason*, I'm going to find out what city you're really from and what you're doing here,' he threatens.

Ren chooses to ignore him, and instead moves his bag off of his bed and on to the floor, lying back down on his bed before putting his arms behind his head and closing his eyes and relaxing his body. However, I can spot the tension in his neck. My skills at reading bodies are more advanced than others, so I doubt the other recruits have noticed.

Apparently deciding to drop the issue, Ian heads back to his bunk. Everyone else moves about the room, some sitting down on their beds, others going to use the bathroom, and the rest simply settling in and making small talk. Harvey and I sit on my bunk across from Lewis.

'Thank you, for sticking up for me, Lewis,' I say.

He smiles faintly, 'No problem, what he said was totally out of line. Surely, no one even thinks that. I mean, I don't think that about you.' He abruptly stops talking, unsure how to finish.

'It's okay. And thank you... for not thinking that of me.'

I cannot help but retreat inside my head to process what had just happened. Why hadn't Ren wanted to tell us where he came from? What is he trying to hide? He stepped in to protect Lewis, which told me that he's a good person. Not many people would stand up for somebody they had never met before. But still, what is he hiding? *And why can't I read him?*

Whatever it was, I had to figure it out before Ian did. If Ian somehow found out whatever it is Ren is hiding, it would only be a matter of time before he used that information against him. I felt I owed it to him to prevent that from happening; after all, he did protect Lewis who was only try-ing to protect me. I would have to keep a close eye on Ian. I could tell he's the type to stab someone in the back the second he gets the chance. He could be a major problem for me.

My train of thought is interrupted as the dormitory door clicks open and the male officer from earlier walks into the room. I jump to my feet and stand at attention.

'If you would all like to follow me, I will lead you to the mess hall for lunch,' he turns on his heel and walks back out of the room, not waiting to see if we follow.

I'm the first to follow the male officer out into the hall-way. We are led back down the hallway to the door that leads to the stairwell we had taken earlier.

He takes us up two flights of stairs and backs out into another identical hallway. We turn left and walk a short distance down the hallway before I begin to hear the chat-tering noise of conversations and laughter. We follow the officer to the end of the hallway and through a set out double doors and into the mess hall. Slowly but surely, I am making a map of the compound in my mind.

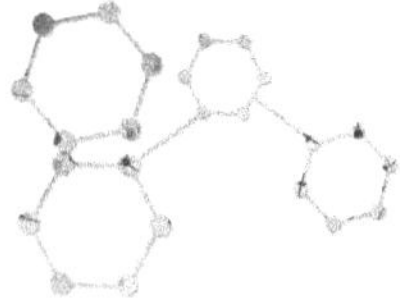

FIVE

THE MESS HALL is a whirl of noise, as cutlery and plates clatter and chairs scrape the floor.

The male officer leads us along the far wall, past rows of tables filled with other recruits until he stops short at a table along the back wall of the mess hall.

'This is the table for Alpha dormitory,' he states. 'You will eat your meals at this table, and this table alone. You may eat now; I will be back on the hour.' With a curt nod, he turns and walks away, leaving us to fend for ourselves.

'Shall we go line up for food?' Harvey suggests to me with a shrug and we make our way over to the opposite side of the mess hall where there is already a line of people waiting to be served their food.

We pick up our trays from the stack at the end of the line and proceed to join the line with the others from our dorm. I am surprised at the assortment of options to choose from: ingredients to make your own hamburger, lasagne, chips, cuts of roast meat and chicken, roast vegetables, salad, the list goes on. It is not the sort of food I had anticipated we would be eating for the next six months. Surely, it must be a last meal of sorts before our training begins. After that, I imagine we will be eating bland and tasteless food that does little more than satisfying our daily nutrient requirements.

I pick up a slice of lasagne, pile on a few chips and then pick some salad. I grab a bottle of water before waiting for Harvey to finish piling food on his plate. I think he realises that this is the last meal too because he piles as much food as he possibly can fit onto his plate. I smile and shake my head at him as he joins me and we head back over to our dorm table and sit down to eat.

Though it is not planned, we all sit in the order of our choice of beds; Harvey sits next to me, with Lewis on his left, followed by Ren.

Unfortunately, this means that I have to sit directly across from Ian. I deliberately angle myself closer to Harvey so that I do not have to look Ian in the eyes while I eat. I don't think I can tolerate looking at his face for the next hour, let alone the next six months.

All the boys at the table have piled as much food as possible onto their trays, either they were all big eaters or they are trying to make the most of their last meal. Skai, not surprisingly, has chosen a slice of chicken and mostly salad for her lunch. No wonder she is so lean. I wonder how she even got accepted.

Harvey and I eat in silence, which gives me the opportunity to observe the rest of the mess hall and the other tables of recruits that arrived while we were off getting our food.

I can see no other female recruits at the other tables, which tells me that Skai and I are it as far as female recruits are concerned. Two females chosen out of one hundred, seems almost ludicrous. This means that there must be something incredibly special about Skai for her to have been chosen. But, when I profile her, I cannot find anything that stands out; she seems like an ordinary girl. But then again, *so do I.*

But, if we are the only two females, then it's likely she will see me as a rival, a potential threat—from experience

I had learned that girls can be incredibly savage with their competitiveness.

I finish eating before Harvey, and have to wait for him to finish his mountain of food before we can head over and place our trays back. Unsure of what to do with the remaining time, we head back over to our table and take our seats again to wait for the male officer. So far, I have not observed one potential ally.

The male officer returns on the hour, he stands at the end of our row and motions for us all to follow. We stand, and the room is filled with the sound of our chairs scraping. We are led back out into the hallway. We head down one flight of stairs. He leads us down the right passage of the hallway until we reach a set of double doors that slide open upon his approach. There is no requirement for a security access card to gain entry into this room.

We follow the officer through the doors and into a large training room, almost the size of a warehouse. The training room has a large aisle down the middle and is broken off into different sections of various training stations. The station closest has large padded matts placed on the floor, with spares braced against the wall for practicing hand to hand combat—at least I assume.

The next training station on the opposite side of the isle is separated into two parts. The first part has targets mounted along the far wall—twenty of them in total—and along the wall next to the station, is an assortment of knives and blades. Knife-throwing practice, I guess. The second part has fake buildings and walls that appear to be crumbling to pieces. I have no idea how they managed to get such lifelike buildings inside this room or this facility. I cannot understand or predict what the buildings could be for and that irritates me.

I drag my attention away from the crumbling buildings and follow the male officer as he leads us down the rest of the long aisle. I take note of the remaining training stations. Along the opposite side of the training room, there are twenty targets mounted on the wall, and just next to it, there are all sorts of guns mounted on the walls. Shooting practice.

It, too, has a second part to it. Crumbling buildings and walls stand next to the target shooting section, and it finally dawns on me what these sections must be used for. I feel stupid for not guessing it sooner.

They are lifelike target practice, because, if we were to be sent into the field, we would be searching through old abandoned buildings and cities, we would not be shooting a target directly in front of us. We would have to learn to cover ourselves from all angles. This is the next level kind of target practice. Exactly what I need.

He leads us to a small section of the training room that is behind the fake buildings. It looks like a space designated for refreshments. Towels, first aid supplies and benches to sit on. There is also a door along the wall, but I don't know where it could lead.

'This is one of the three training rooms you will be using over the next six months.' As the officer speaks, his voice echoes around the training room.

'As you can see, there are three different training stations set up in this particular room. They are for hand-to-hand combat and sparring, knife throwing and knife work, and shooting,' he counts the three stations off on his fingers as he spoke. 'The buildings that are next to each station are designed for a more in-depth kind of training. When training inside these buildings, you will be tested by stimulation. That stimulation will create Genesi that will appear at random and it will be your job to ensure that you kill each and every one of them. If you miss just one, you will fail.

'Through this room,' he turns to point at the door on the wall behind him, 'you will find a hallway that leads to two sets of classrooms. The first door on the left is where you will be taught first aid and survival training, and the second room is where you will be taught in greater detail about the Genesi, their history and why we send soldiers outside the walls.'

'On the level directly above us, is another training room. The room's perimeter allows for running laps, while its centre is an obstacle course designed to test your fitness and teamwork skills.

'There are seven stations in total, and each one will teach you valuable skills that you will need to survive out in the field. Each unit will be paired with another unit, and everyone will rotate through the stations on a daily basis. You will all begin your mornings running drills upstairs, after which you will complete training at one of the stations for the remainder of the morning. After lunch, you will complete training at another station. You may utilise the rec room after training in the evening, both before and after dinner. You must be in your dormitories by lights out. When you return to your dormitories this afternoon, you will find a map on each of your bunks that details the places you will be required to know in this training facility. I suggest you familiarise yourself quickly.'

Excitement fills me. *They are giving us a map.* It's doubtful that it will have much information on it, but if it can give me some greater understanding of the layout of this place, it will make my plans much easier.

'In a moment, Chancellor Cain and General Thorn will be meeting us to assess you, debrief you and answer a few of your questions. I expect I don't have to warn you to behave.'

Cain. If I can just get him to answer some questions, it might be enough to help set my plans in motion. I will just have to hope that Harvey clues in and can help cover for me if need be.

The doors we came through into the training room open suddenly. We all turn to face the two men walking towards the group. I instantly recognise Cain. Today, he is wearing a navy blue suit with a white button-down shirt and a slim navy blue tie. His gaze is set dead ahead with a detached sort of determination, almost as if he were bored.

Chancellor Cain and the general stop in front of the group, standing beside the male officer who stiffly turns and walks back towards the entry doors, stopping to stand at attention. No, *on guard.*

'Good afternoon, recruits,' Chancellor Cain addresses us, his voice void of any emotion. 'I would like to introduce you to General Thorn.' Cain gestures to the general with his right hand. General Thorn does not move; he remains standing at attention alongside the chancellor, staring dead ahead into the middle of the group and choosing to look at no one in particular.

'We would like to congratulate you all on being accepted and chosen to train with the hope to become a member of Delta Force. Only the best applicants are chosen to be recruited into this special task force. Should you succeed with your training, you will be deployed into the field and sent on covert missions outside these walls. There, you will track and gather valuable intelligence on the whereabouts of any remaining Genesi, as well as gathering valuable scientific data that is crucial in our developments of the cure. I will leave it to General Thorn to explain in greater detail what is expected of you.' He stands back and General Thorn moves from attention to address the group. Cain's eyes seek me out and catch my gaze before I can look away. Instead of holding his gaze, I quickly turn my attention to the general. *Let him think I am afraid of him.*

General Thorn is tall with broad shoulders and is in incredible physical shape for someone who appears in his late forties. He has a dominating presence that is contributed to by his stiff, formal posture and the hard set of his jaw as he gazes at the group. His hair is closely cropped to his scalp and is black with a few greying areas towards the front. His skin is tanned from excessive exposure from the sun. He looks familiar; though, I am sure I've never laid eyes upon him before.

In profiling General Thorn, I learn very little. His behaviour demonstrates that he has had much practice over the years at making himself unreadable. The only characteristic that I am able to detect is malice. This man is a violent man.

His voice is deep and emotionless as he addresses the recruits. 'As you know, you are here because you want to do your part in assisting in freeing our country from the Genesi. You know what the Genesi are and how they were created, and I want to ensure that you understand the full magnitude of your being here.' He stops to assess the crowd; his eyes linger on me briefly before continuing with his speech.

'One hundred years ago, a World War occurred, the Genesi began changing, they became less and less in control of themselves, less humane. They attacked anyone in their path, soldiers from their own country, country leaders, innocent civilians, causing thousands upon thousands of deaths. The Genesi became bloodthirsty savages that the governments could no longer control.

'The United Nations held a meeting where they agreed that the Genesi posed too great of a threat and that they needed to be eradicated. The Genesi Coding program was disbanded immediately.

'No one was prepared for when the Genesi struck first with bombs of their own, killing millions. The war became so catastrophic that the best option the governments could find was to barricade themselves and their civilians inside their cities. They bombed the remaining lands with strategic nuclear force. Those that remained outside were either killed by the force of the explosions or radiation poisoning. Most of the land outside the walls was destroyed by radiation, making it impossible to live on, even today.

The United Nations agreed that it would be safest to remain inside the city walls, as the outside world was rendered uninhabitable. But then came the second wave of Genesi. The damage dealt nearly rendered the human race extinct. They broke through our walls with their supernatural strength and invaded our cities, killing all they found in their path. The only solution foreseeable was to bomb those invaded cities.

'Over time, our ancestors made our walls stronger, developing a force field that would surround the cities along with the wall, creating an even stronger barricade against any remaining Genesi.

'Over the last one hundred years, we have remained inside the walls that our ancestors built. Our society now thrives and we have scientists working non-stop towards developing a cure for the Genesi coding. *However,* it has been over a century and still, we have been unable to find one. This is why our Delta Force is so vital to our survival.

'It's the main reason you are all here today. Until a cure is found, we must continue to monitor and track the Genesi. Their location is vital knowledge for when a cure is found. You will be required to track and monitor the Genesi, observe their behaviour and report all of your findings back to base. The most important information we need to obtain is where they are hiding and how they are surviving on such poisoned land.

'Unfortunately, only twenty of you will make it into the Delta Force. You were each selected based on your strengths that were identified during your aptitude test. Each and every one of you has been assessed as being one of the best of the best. No one is here for the same reason as the person standing next to them.' At this, the general looks towards me.

'You have been divided into units of ten, each unit has an assortment of different strengths and you have been placed in your units based on your rankings. You will be taught both theoretical and physical application in your training, but it is vital that you learn to work *together*; working *with* your unit ensures your survival outside in the field.

'In your theory training, you will undertake constant testing in order to continually re-evaluate your rankings; in your physical training, you will also be assessed, however, you will be assessed on accuracy, strength, speed and durability. Remember, it's not about who wins the fight, but who shows the best skills during the fight.' The general steps back, leaving us to consider his message.

Chancellor Cain clears his throat noisily. 'You will be given your rankings at the end of each month, however, by the end of the six-month long training, if you do not rank in the top twenty, you will not become a member of Delta Force.

'We will remain to answer your questions, and then you will be escorted back to your dormitories, so please, start asking straightaway,' he gestures with his hand for us to proceed with questions, but nobody dares speak, no one wants to be the first to ask.

This is your chance, Luka; you won't get a second one. I clear my throat, 'What of the cure?' I ask. 'How far away are we from discovering one?' I am grateful for how clear my voice sounds.

'Ah yes, excellent question, Private Foster,' the chancellor holds my gaze as he speaks, almost daring me to ask the one question I so desperately want to ask. 'So far, we are no closer to developing a cure than we were one hundred years ago. We have managed to observe the genetic changes in the Genesi over time and this is what we believe to be the problem. The Genesi are evolving, you see, the coding in their DNA appears different than what it did originally, and this makes it incredibly difficult to develop a cure.'

His words ring false in my ears. He is not telling me anything that I hadn't already worked out.

I had predicted this years before, that the Genesi had evolved and that they were not the same as they were when they were first created. But in what way were they changing? Were they becoming more human? Or were they becoming something worse?

I have to ask, let him think that I have taken the bait.

'In what way are they evolving, Sir?'

Cain smiles at my question before he answers as if he knows the reason I would need to know the answer, 'It would appear that they are becoming more and more savage, Private Foster, they are becoming a greater danger to us all.'

'Wouldn't it be best if we just killed them all?' asks Ian. I cringe at the obnoxious tone

A heartbeat passes. 'We are not *savages* like our ancestors were,' Cain answers, bemused. 'We as humans, try to look for the most humane solution, something that our ancestors failed to do. We have to remember that the Genesi were once human beings just like us, to kill them all would make us no better than them, a mistake our ancestors made.

Thanks to the Genesi, the human race is on the brink of extinction, but we can change that.'

There was a sombre silence throughout the room as everyone reflected upon Cain's answer. I try to process the chancellor's words, but his words and his behaviour are at war with one another. He speaks of wanting to cure the Genesi, wanting to save our lands and our people. But a man who wants all of that would not commission the re-development of the Genesi coding. My evaluating thoughts are interrupted as somebody asks another question.

The voice is husky with a hint of defiance when it asks, 'What would happen then if we were in the field and were discovered and our position compromised. What if we were backed into a corner and it was fight or flight? What would be the more *humane* thing to do, to kill the Genesi or to let ourselves be killed by them? And what if it were a member of our unit, do we just leave them behind?' His question holds hints of malice and an underlying threat. It appears that Ren is just as suspicious of Chancellor Cain as I am. After all, why else would he ask for answers about what happened to the chancellor's son?

Chancellor Cain takes a moment to formulate his response.

I notice General Thorn staring at Ren, looking at him with such an obvious hatred, proving I am right about the underlying malice and violence in this man. But Ren returns his gaze and holds it. There was no malice in his eyes, only defiance.

Though we have only just met the general, judging from their body language, it becomes clear that they already know each other. *How do they already know each other?*

Ren had asked this particular question for a reason, and whatever reason that may be, it appears that he is getting the response he wanted. The recruits are starting to become restless, questioning. Both the chancellor and the general are struggling to regain control.

'That is,' begins Cain slowly, 'a very difficult question to answer. The senate and I have always been opposed to the killing of innocent life, and, personally, I feel as though, despite what the Genesi have done to us in the past, and what we in turn have done to them, killing them off would be inhumane, wrong even.'

'I believe that curing them would be the most *humane* solution. But you are right in pointing out that it is not always so black and white. There are circumstances where we must put aside our humanity and our beliefs for the good of mankind. In this particular instance, sacrificing one or two Genesi or even one member of your unit to save the lives of your entire unit so that we might find a cure would be more humane.

'I believe that in the circumstance that you are referring to, it would be a decision that you would need to make, not for yourself, but the good of mankind. And that is what you will be trained to do, to think not of yourselves, but of our country, of the civilians who are in danger each and every day, and I know you, like my son, will make the right decision when the time is right.'

Liar. Liar. Liar.

'If it were you in this particular situation, Chancellor Cain, what would you do? What decision would you make if you were in our shoes?' I know it's risky, I don't even need to look at Harvey next to me to know he is struggling to keep the shock of my boldness off of his face. Horrified at me for asking such a question and annoyed that I have brought such attention to myself.

I can feel the tension among the crowd; feel people shift uncomfortably on their feet as we waited for Cain's response.

I can hear Ian sniggering in the background, clearly expecting me to be reprimanded for asking such a question. *Maybe I will be.*

To my surprise, Chancellor Cain chuckles. It unnerves me. He does not find my question humorous. He knows why I am asking because I want him to lie to me. I need him to lie and tell me that he had nothing to do with my father's death. *But we both know that he did.*

'If I were to find myself in such a situation,' he begins after some time, he looks me directly in the eyes as he speaks, a cruel knowing in his eyes, 'if it were me and I was backed into a corner, I would do whatever it took to ensure that my unit survived.' *Bastard.*

He chuckles again as he catches the crowd by surprise, 'but thankfully, you will all be given sufficient training and I dare say it is doubtful you should find yourself in such a dire situation.'

'What will happen if our rankings aren't good enough to make it into Delta Force, what will happen to us then?'

I had no idea who the voice belonged to, it sounded like it was several rows behind me.

It is General Thorn who addresses this question head on, 'It will depend upon your rankings. If you have ranked higher in your physical assessments, it is likely that you will be moved to a different department within our military. If you have ranked somewhat in the middle, it is likely you might find yourself becoming a member of our police force and sent to a city that has a position vacant. And, if you rank higher in the intellectual aspect of things, then it is likely you might find yourself in a different job description or education altogether, as clearly, your knowledge is better served elsewhere.

'What of rankings for female recruits?' I ask. 'I mean,

very few females in history have made it into Delta Force, and those that have were never deployed into the field. How are we to be ranked?'

It's a dangerous question to ask, but I *need* to know. No female has been sent out into the field and I felt compelled to know why. My plans are riding on making it outside the wall. The likelihood of being the first female ever to be deployed in the field was incredibly low and it agonised me that I could not figure out why that was. I *need* to be deployed into the field; all of my plans were counting on it.

'Such an interesting question,' Cain drawls, 'we had only two successful females this year, both yourself, Private Foster along with Private Mendez. The first reason why such a small percentage makes it through the applications is firstly, because not many females are able to pass the very specific aptitude test.

'Most females, like I said, do not pass the aptitude test. Those that do, they undergo the same training and assessing as a male would. Whether or not they can rank higher than a male is up to the individual female. It is common knowledge that females are generally physically weaker than men.'

Pig.

He looks directly at me, trying to hold my gaze. I hold it right back.

'I in no way wish to sound sexist, Private Foster.'

We both know that's a lie.

'But it is scientifically proven that women are generally physically weaker than men. That being said, women often rank the highest in our intellectual assessments, which is just as important as the physical assessments; *however*, their overall rankings are lowered because of their poorer physical results.

'I would strongly advise that if you wish to be accepted

into the Delta Force, you will concentrate dearly on both your physical, as well as your theory training, as ranking assessments begin from day one. Every day counts, Private Foster.' He adds dryly.

'If the best way to survive out in the field was to work efficiently as a unit and rely on one another's strengths, wouldn't it be beneficial to have at least one female in the unit? As you said, they might not rank as high as a male, but females also think very differently from men, their thought process is often sharper and their decision-making skills, as well as their ability to think outside of regulations, would be a valuable asset to any unit. Perhaps the reason why so many soldiers have been killed or not returned is precisely that no females are allowed into the field.' It was Harvey this time. I clenched my jaw to control my frustration that he had come to my defence. I had to work really hard to not let it show on my face.

There is a mixture of sniggers throughout the crowd; I recognise Ian among them. Others shift uncomfortably. At least they know better than to talk back to Harvey in front of the chancellor. But, once we returned to our dorm, I knew it would come up.

Better that they think I am weak.

Cain waits a few moments until the crowd has settled before acknowledging Harvey's question; his face was a mask, carefully controlled as he speaks.

'That is a valid argument you make there, Private. Actually, that has been considered in the past; however, it would be unfair to allow someone with lower rankings into Delta Force over somebody with the required ranks, don't you agree?'

'But can't the senate just lower the percentile for female rankings to be more fairly ranked?' I butt in. I just catch

Chancellor Cain's jaw tighten before he quickly regains his resolve.

'If only it were that simple, Private Foster,' he says calmly. 'And now, I think that is enough questions for today. I can see that we have chosen an excellent array of applicants this year. And I believe you will all be well cared for under the watchful eye of General Thorn.

'Recruits, if you would please follow Captain Malik, he will escort you back to your dormitories or to the recreational room where you may spend the remainder of your day, your training will begin 0600 hours tomorrow.'

People began to slowly turn to follow the male officer, Captain Malik, out of the training facility.

'Oh, and Private Foster, if I could have but a minute of your time.' Cain barely contains the slyness in his voice.

My stomach is instantly filled with dread.

Damn.

Perhaps I really am going to be reprimanded for my questions.

I feel my heart racing. I hear my pulse in my ears as my hands became slick with sweat as my chest tightens. *Panic.* That's what is happening to me. The anxiety threatens to take control once more. I take steady, even breaths.

I watch as everyone begins to file out of the room, and soon the doors are closing behind them. I am left alone with Cain and Thorn. The only two men in this world that could kill me and convince society that they were the victims.

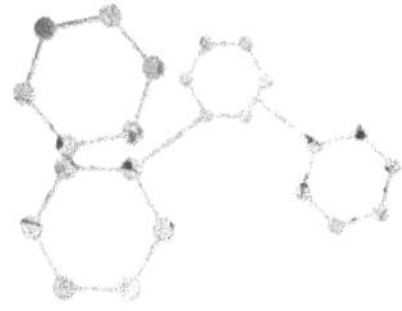

SIX

'TELL ME, PRIVATE Foster, why did you apply for Delta Force?' Cain asks me. He speaks with forced politeness and it is obvious he already knows the answer to his question. His face is a perfect mask of control and I can see just how hard he is working to keep it that way. I sense that there is a perfectly controlled temper underneath his perfect façade; a temper I had caused simply because I had overstepped.

I wonder if anybody else saw him, really *saw* him, for who he was. Did they notice that despite the calm, polite manner he presents, there is a tension in his jaw from gritting his teeth together and tightness in his eyes? Though he faces me directly, I can see that his back is tense, the muscles pulled together tightly. There is a swirling storm cloud of anger, pooling underneath. My father had been right to fear him.

Thorn is still standing next to him, watching me with an almost predator-like gaze, his dark eyes boring into mine. I could sense the underlying malice.

The chancellor waits for my answer, so I take one final long breath to control my nerves before I lie directly in the face of the devil.

'I joined with the hope to be the first female deployed, Sir,' I speak clearly and force as much politeness as I can into my voice to hide the lie.

Cain smiled; the movement looked unnatural on his face. *He knows that I lied. He's already guessed the true reason I am here. Was I that obvious?* There has to be a chance I can still fix this. He can't know that I suspect him, or General Thorn.

'Also...' I hesitate and swallow, enough to make it look as if this was difficult to talk about, to admit to him. 'Also, I want to learn more about the Genesi. My...my father, he was close, *so close* to finding a way to cure them. I would like to see my father's work finished.' My voice quickly becomes raspy; I do not have an act too emotional when talking about my father. I just have to hope it is enough to convince him.

Bringing up my father seemed to be the right move. Cain's eyes seem to lighten as he takes in my words.

'Your father was a good man. He was dedicated, he was driven and he was our best chance at a cure. Our progress has been at somewhat of a standstill since your father's death.'

'What do you mean at a standstill?' I ask, trying to appear innocent.

'I mean, for more than one hundred years, scientists and geneticists have been working to find a cure. In that period of one hundred years, no scientific mind has ever been as advanced as Christopher Foster's. Because of that, he was our highest hope.'

My father had been incredibly smart; he had one of the highest recorded IQs in history.

'I will admit,' Cain went on, 'I had hoped that you would follow in your father's footsteps and join our geneticists division, perhaps even complete your father's work; you would have very easily met the criteria for it.'

He was baiting me.

'For a long while, I did want to join the geneticist team,' I said. 'I thought that if I did, I could somehow finish what he had started. But, it became clear to me that perhaps the reason why he was never able to finish the cure was because he had spent his entire life in a lab, studying Genesi that had been captured or reading reports and data from soldiers that have no scientific understanding of the data that they were collecting. And, it occurred to me, maybe that is where he had gone wrong. What if, by studying them firsthand, in their natural habitat, learning how they have survived on land that is poisoned, I would have a better chance at seeing what everyone has been missing, and perhaps I could apply that to my father's formula.'

Some of that is true; I had always thought that the reason why they couldn't figure out a cure was because they were looking at data from soldiers who had no understanding of science. Or possibly that the data they were obtaining from captured Genesi was inadequate. They would be able to see evolved DNA, but they wouldn't have a clear understanding of *why* it had evolved. Their lifestyle, diet, reproduction... all those things could fundamentally contribute to their evolution. Understanding why they were evolving was vital. My father knew that too. And I suspect that he would have also wanted to learn how they were surviving on land that was supposedly poisoned.

Finding a cure and finishing my father's work had always been a part of my plan. It just was not my number one priority. First, I had to find out why somebody wanted my father dead, and how it relates to the Genesi project he was working on. First, I had to avenge my father, only then I could work towards ending the Genesi war.

I sensed that Cain knew what happened the day that my father died.

'That... is an interesting theory, Private Foster. Tell me, General Thorn, what are your thoughts on this theory?' He says with a coy smile that makes my blood boil.

General Thorn clears his throat, 'I believe it is an interesting theory... certainly something... unheard of.'

'And do you think it is a theory that we should be testing... considering?'

'I am not entirely sure, Sir; perhaps a question better asked that of a scientist or geneticist. She certainly needs evidence to prove her claim.'

'Yes, I believe you are right. Tell me, Private Foster, if you were to be deployed into the field, what would you do differently? How would you survive? How would you return, when others before you have not?'

A test.

'Because I am *female* and because I am Christopher Foster's daughter, *Sir.*'

Cain chuckles lightly, Thorn, however, does not look impressed. It becomes clear that he does not approve of my presence here. I am unsure if it is because I am female or if it is because of my father. Perhaps both.

Thorn strikes me as the kind of man that does not approve of female soldiers, that he feels they belong in the home completing domestic duties and raising children and not in the military protecting fellow soldiers and this country.

He also strikes me as being Cain's lackey.

'Perhaps you are right, Private Foster, you made a valid argument earlier. I am beginning to think that you are a lot more like your father than I was prepared for.'

'Thank you... Sir.' I feign confusion, for his sake. I need him to keep talking, need him to slip up somewhere.

'You father was somebody who liked to push boundaries—think outside the box, so to speak. It seems that you are designed that way too. I always believed that it was your father's way of thinking that brought him so close, don't you think?' he asks lightly in an attempt to bait me once again.

Or, it was your doing that brought him so close, don't you think?

I choose to say nothing. There is a moment of tense silence as he waits for my response that will not come.

'So tell me then, *Private* Foster.' The way he says my name, the way he pronounces 'Private', it's as if the word tastes bitter in his mouth. 'Do you think you have what it takes, to survive, return, and then complete your father's work?' He challenges.

I see the right side of his mouth twitching as if he were straining not to laugh or smile, he thinks he has me wrapped around his finger. The rest of his face is the perfectly controlled mask; only the twitching gives him away.

'I think I do, Sir.'

'And why is that, Private Foster? What makes you think you can do what those before you could not, what your father could not?'

'Precisely what you said, Sir; I am my father's daughter. I have my father's ability to think differently to others, I have an IQ higher than my father's and I have trained myself and my body to be capable of surviving.'

'Yes, indeed you have,' he muses. 'Your test results were most impressive, don't you think, General?'

General Thorn clears his throat. 'Yes, I was quite surprised to see how high you tested in all fields, both physically and intellectually.'

'Most peculiar, wasn't it? To see somebody, test so well in all the fields,' Cain drawls sarcastically. Either he knows something, or he suspects something.

'I was not aware I scored so well, Sir,' I answer, cutting off Thorn before he has the chance to speak.

I am aware that he is trying to unnerve me, make me nervous enough that I give myself away.

'Yes, you had the highest test scores we had ever seen in an applicant. You must have trained incredibly hard, must have been incredibly... *dedicated.*'

He knows. He knows why I am here.

The anxiety threatens to take over. My lungs start to burn. I try to read him—re-assess the situation and calm myself down. He knows I am here to avenge my father's death, to find his killer. But he does not know the entire reason why I am here. That much is clear, but he is trying to guess. And, so far, no matter how much he tries to manipulate the truth out of me, he is not even close to knowing the truth.

Good. I feel the tightness in my chest lessen and I can breathe easily again.

'I spent the last few years training for this, with the hope that my theory would pay off. But, that would depend, wouldn't it, on whether or not I get deployed.'

I will play his little game. If he thinks manipulating me to get answers will work, then let's see if the same will work for him.

'I see. You want to know if you will be deployed.' He pauses, thinking. 'Well, Private Foster, you will have to prove your worth. Prove to me that you can keep yourself alive, first.'

Damn. He's good.

He knows I am playing the game too. I have to try to slow my racing heart and keep my composure. I cannot let him see how much he has shaken me. I have to give him what he wants to get what I want.

'I can keep myself alive; I have so far, haven't I? I mean... whoever murdered my father tried to hurt me too—perhaps even tried to kill me. I am still alive, aren't I?' I swallow and make myself look nervous, scared, which is easy to do, as my heart is still beating like a humming bird.

'Yes… you are quite the survivor.' His eyes gleam.

'My father wasn't working on the cure, was he? It was something else, and that's what got him killed.'

'A good guess, Private Foster. Although it is strictly confidential, I feel it is best if you know the truth. Or at least part of it.'

I take a deep breath to make sure no emotion registers on my face.

'Your father was initially assigned to the cure, to work on developing it and implementing it. After your father died, there was an investigation and inquiry, naturally. It was discovered that your father had been utilising the data and studies of the cure to work on something else entirely.

'We were unable to decipher what specifically it was that your father had been working on, only that it was likely he was attempting to re-create the Genesi Coding; for what end, we cannot be sure. Your father's behaviour had changed significantly towards the end; he was elusive and paranoid, I am sorry to say.'

Liar. My blood boils.

My father had left me a recording of the night before he died. It cuts out after a few minutes, but he says in his recording that Cain was the one who had commissioned him to work on the cure, and then later commissioned him to work on the re-development of the Genesi Coding. Cain wanted it recreated, so that new soldiers who were genetically modified would be susceptible to suggestion, that they could be controlled by him.

I believe my father. I would never doubt him.

Cain clearly is the most obvious suspect; he had motive and resources. He may not have been the one who pulled the trigger, but it is likely he commissioned the kill. And I'd bet my arse that the lackey he commissioned to kill my father was Thorne.

But, if Cain *had* commissioned my father's death, was it because my father had completed his work for him and he wanted to silence him? Or was it because my father had *refused* to complete his work and been killed because of it? Was it something else entirely? These are the questions that keep me up at night.

Now that they know how close I am to the truth, I will have to proceed with caution. They will have me watched at all times and this will complicate things. I need more information before I can make my next move.

For now, I will play along with their game and let them believe that they are winning. I will play their game of cards, but they shall not know that I am the joker.

'I see.' I clear my throat and hesitate for effect, 'I was not aware of my father's behaviour, or of what he had been working on.' The lie tastes bitter in my mouth.

Cain smiles—it's malicious and smug. 'But of course, you could not have been aware; you were just a young child all those years ago,' he reconciles, forcing a look of mournfulness into his expression.

Prick.

I flick my gaze to Thorn; he too is forcing himself to look saddened at the accusations regarding my father with his head bowed and eyes hooded.

I let them think I believe them. Let them think that they have my trust.

'Nevertheless,' Cain continues, 'it is best if we put these dark times and thoughts behind us, where they belong. Instead, we should be focusing on the present and on the future. I believe you will make a great asset, Private Foster.

I believe that despite your father's dark past, you might be able to write his wrong doings, and with working alongside General Thorn and myself, bring our people to salvation. What do you say, Private Foster?'

Work with them and they will give me the answers I need—I can do that.

'I look forward to working with you, Sir, both of you.' I force a smile and it makes my face hurt.

Cain's smile is that of a cat that has just caught a mouse. He could not be more wrong, I was no mouse to be trapped by a cat, I am the fox that has gotten into the chicken coop.

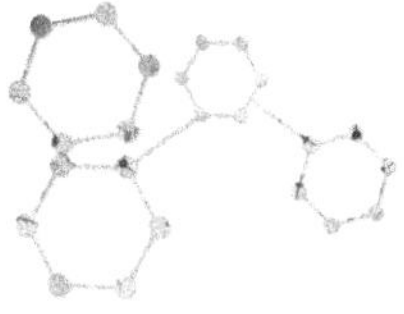

SEVEN

THE DORM IS almost empty when I return. Only Harvey is inside, lying on his bed, eyes closed, with his arms propped behind his head.

'Where is everyone?' I ask, stepping into the dorm.

Harvey leaps from his bunk and comes to stand in front of me. His eyebrows are drawn inwards, concerned. 'I waited for you. What happened?'

I breathe out a heavy sigh. 'It's a long story.'

'Everyone is in the rec room, so, we have time.'

I scan the room, making sure there are no obvious cameras or voice recording devices hidden anywhere. I walk over and sit down on my bunk, my hands folded loosely in my lap, and take a deep breath. I tell him everything.

'Do you think that Chancellor Cain had something to do with you getting in here?' Harvey asks eventually.

'It's entirely possible,' I reply. 'Based on the conversations I've had with him, I certainly wouldn't rule out the possibility. Plus, he did say that he wanted me to work with him...' I shrug.

'But work with him to what end? What does he want from you?' Harvey likes where this is headed about as much as I do.

'I think that he is hoping that I can finish my father's

work, finish re-developing the Genesi Coding. I get the impression that my father wanted no part in it and that he was killed to ensure his silence. I think Cain is searching for someone else who is willing to work on re-developing it. I think he is hoping that with me, it will not end like it did for my father.'

'Do you think…'

I sigh. 'Just say it,'

He exhales roughly. 'Do you think it could be possible that maybe your father was all for re-developing the Genesi Coding at the beginning, but then changed his mind towards the end? I mean, we really don't know what happened back then.'

'You mean, do I think my father was ever okay with the idea of creating a formula to genetically alter a human's DNA, a formula that created the largest war in history so that our corrupt leader could use it to his own ends? No, I do not.' I snap, struggling to regain control of my breathing.

How could he even think that? How could anybody ever think that? My father was a good man; he was kind, honest and open. He was not capable of such cruelty. And to even think that, just for a second, felt like a betrayal of his memory.

'You're right; your father was a good man… sorry.'

I brush off his apology; I can't let my emotions get in the way of my mission anymore. 'We need to focus on our training. For what it's worth, it will be the most valuable information we learn here.'

'Okay… what else? I mean, you realise now would be a good time to share the rest of your plan with me. Instead of keeping me in the dark like you always do.'

'I keep you in the dark about my plans to keep you safe, not because I don't trust you.'

'I know,' he sighs. 'Just tell me what we need to do next.'

'We need to start mapping out this facility. I have already mapped out the areas we have been to in my head, but I want to write them down for us both, in case we need it. Then we need to map as much of this place as we can,' I say.

'Right, well, we can use this,' he adds, holding up a small floor plan. It only included the dorm rooms, mess hall, training rooms and what I guessed was the rec room. I then noticed that I had a copy on my own bunk. *It's all too perfect.*

'First, we will use these maps to complete mapping the rest of the facility.'

'That's the easy part,' he mutters.

'Then we need to find someone who is capable of hacking into a computer system... somebody with great computer skills.' I risk a glance at him. 'Somebody like Lewis.'

'No, absolutely not. You can't be serious,' he says loudly, rising to his feet.

'I am, unfortunately. He is the only one with the necessary skills. I just don't know if we can convince him to help us, which is why we need to make a plan B. We need to profile everybody: recruits, trainers, anybody. We need to find somebody else that is capable of hacking a computer system. We need to look for some allies,' I conclude.

Harvey slowly sinks back down. 'Okay, so we are looking for somebody *else* who is good with computers?'

I nod my affirmation.

'I take it you want me to get close to Lewis?' Harvey asks, frustration leaking into his voice. 'I mean, because you are so approachable and all.'

'I am approachable,' I argue, knowing that he's right.

'No, you're not,' he chuckles and then sobers, 'People find you too intense and intimidating.'

I roll my eyes. 'Whatever; just get close to him and

anyone else you think is good with computers, or anybody that I tell you to.'

'Yes, Sir,' he mock salutes, and then he adds gingerly, 'I also think we should watch our backs with Ian—you specifically. I have a feeling he is going to try something, after what happened this morning. To be honest, I'm surprised he hasn't already. You really pissed him off.'

'I know.' I sigh. 'We need to watch him, and Skai too. I think those two will become allies if they aren't already. We need to ensure neither one of them rats us out. Or gangs up on us.'

'And what about the other kid... Ren?' Harvey gauges my reaction. 'I think we should keep an eye out for him too. Something just doesn't feel right about him.'

He is right in a way, Ren is a mystery. A mystery I have an unusual desire to unravel. For some reason I can't explain, I'm dying to know more about him, so far he has not been exactly forthcoming with information about himself. I sense that he keeps the same kind of walls in place that I do. That just makes the urge to figure him out that much more compelling.

'I don't think he is dangerous, if that's what you're getting at.' I say eventually. 'But I do think we should find out more about him. He *is* hiding something, and I need to know what it is.'

'Yeah well, don't expect me to get close to him,' he grumbles. 'Because I don't think even a wrecking ball could break through those walls.'

I smile. 'Just you wait and see. Will you show me the rec room? I need to check a few things.'

'Sure,' he jumps up from his bunk.

* * *

THE REC ROOM is much larger than I expect. It is about the size of a gymnasium or hall. It is sectioned off into smaller areas by collapsible, movable partitions.

In one corner, there are several vision screens and couches where I can see other recruits relaxing. I turned my nose up at them. There was never much to watch on those things.

In another corner, I can see old billiard tables. I notice that Ian and Skai are standing next to one of them with cues in their hands, laughing and playing with the others around them. There are also old table tennis tables with a few others playing.

We continue walking through the rec room, heading towards the back. We pass people relaxing on couches and chairs, some chatting with others, some reading. I notice that there are several cameras planted in each corner of the rec room. They are extremely small, just slight variations in the colour on the wall. I doubted that many of the recruits had spotted them.

As we reach the back of the room, we walk through the doorway of one of the collapsible walls and into what appears to be some sort of study or computer lab. There are bookshelves lining the walls. By quickly reading their spines, I notice that the books are mostly for entertainment, not study. There are a series of desks running along the back wall, each with a computer at them. And there, sitting at one of the computers, is Lewis.

Judging from the sounds animating from the computer, he must be playing some form of video game. I can hear gunfire and shouting. Lewis is so fixated on the screen before him that he doesn't even notice us standing behind him.

I watch as Harvey walks over to one of the empty computer desks, hunting through the drawers until he finds what he is looking for. I watch as he grabs a notepad and some pens and pockets them.

I nod to him, and we begin to make our way out of the rec room. On the way out, I notice a lone figure sitting on a lounge chair, his dark hair falling in his eyes that are transfixed on the book he is reading.

I could not see the title, but my curiosity got the better of me.

'What are you reading?' I ask as I stand before him.

Without so much as a glance upwards, he replies, '*The Adventures of Sherlock Holmes.*'

I am surprised. Of all of the books in that room to choose from, he chose one that was several centuries old, and a personal favourite of mine.

'You're a fan of Sir Arthur Conan Doyle?' I ask, eyebrows raised and surprise myself by hoping that his answer is yes.

Ren breathes out a heavy sigh and places the book down in his lap, annoyed.

'Not so much,' he says, crossing his fingers in his lap. 'Though I do enjoy Sherlock Holmes. I enjoy the historical aspect of the story and the character's brilliant mind.'

Me too.

'So you like learning history?'

He gives me a long, measured look as if deciding whether or not to answer my question.

'I enjoy reading about what the world was once like, before the Genesi, when it was filled with so much potential, where the most bizarre invention was a fictional character who could solve crimes, when back then, the possibility of a human being so intelligent was completely unbelievable unless it was only in fiction.' His voice is casual, but I catch his underlying meaning—he wants a world without Genesi.

Don't we all?

'I like reading about that too.' I smile at him.

I am smiling like an idiot. Stop smiling, Luka.

He smiles back at me. It's only a half-smile, with one side of his lips turned up. But it's enough for me to make the sudden realisation that he is incredibly attractive. The smile causes his eyes to light up, and I feel a strange stirring inside.

Stop staring Luka.

He turns his attention back to the book before him, oblivious to the fact that I was still standing there smiling at him like an idiot, or maybe he just didn't care. I could see his brows creased and his lips part slightly in concentration and I decide to leave him be.

I shake my head, clearing away my confusing thoughts and I turn back to Harvey. He is watching me with a bewildered expression and I storm past him as I continue to walk from the rec room, away from any prying eyes and ears.

'What was that about?' he asks me as soon as we turned out into the hallway.

'Nothing,' I say shortly.

'Didn't look like *nothing* to me.'

'And what did it *look* like then?' I challenge.

He gives one long, measured look. 'Nothing,' I hear him mutter.

I had hoped I wouldn't have to deal with this. My observations of people had taught me when others were angry, or happy, or in love... so I wasn't blind to Harvey's feelings. I just wasn't prepared to address them. I refused to analyse my own feelings, knowing that the disruption could possibly mess up not just my plans, but mind.

I know it's selfish, but I need him. I wouldn't handle coping if I ever lost Harvey, he has been the glue that has held the broken pieces of me together since my father died. And, I know that if that glue were to be removed, I would not just fall to pieces again, there would simply be no pieces left of me to piece back together. One thing I did know was that Harvey deserved better. He deserves better than me.

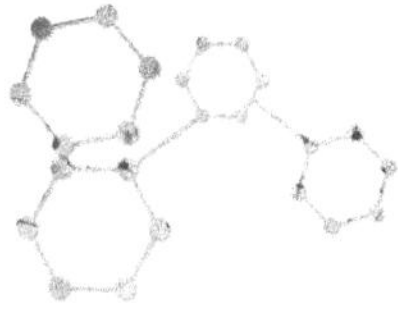

EIGHT

'THE FIRST TRAINING section is hand-to-hand combat training and sparring,' says Captain Wells.

Wells was assigned to my unit, which consists of dorms one and two, this morning, after we ran a series of running drills upstairs in the second training facility. We were woken at 0530 hours this morning by an intercom, advising us to wake up, get dressed, and be in the training rooms by 0600 hours.

Once we were all gathered in the training facility, General Thorn appeared and separated us all into groups of units that consisted of two dormitories. He then assigned us a trainer: Captain Wells.

She is in what I guessed were her mid-thirties, so I knew she was well-seasoned. She's of average height and her body is toned, her muscles hinting at their strength as she moves around us, shouting drills at us. She ran us through a series of running drills to warm us up before the real training began.

I was not able to see much of the facility when travelling to the upstairs training facility, something I am sure was deliberate. We were taken through identical hallways that I have already memorised. Captain Wells informed us, with a flick of her short, sandy blonde ponytail, that later in our training, we would be running these drills outside of the city walls, to better prepare ourselves for when the time came and we were *lucky* enough to be deployed. That spiked a surge of excitement through all of us.

We would be starting with sparring, while the other groups were each assigned to a training station of their own for the morning. In the afternoon, after lunchtime, we would be moving on to what Wells described as 'Basic Survival Skills 101'.

'I will be separating you into relatively evenly matched pairs. Listen up for your partners. Mason with Jenson, Kingston with Montgomery…'

I tune Wells out, only listening with one ear for my name. Excellent, Harvey will be partnered with Lewis. This will give him the chance to get close to him, see if maybe he could convince him to help us, become our ally. It was a long shot, but if anyone could do it, Harvey could.

'And finally, Mendez with Foster.'

Great. I bet they paired me with the only other female because they think we should be equally matched because of our gender. *Idiots.*

'You will not be sparring the entire time you are training in this section. Today, I will select a pair to be assessed in their sparing techniques, those not currently being assessed will practice with their partner, or individually with a bag.' She motions to the wall of punching bags that are hung along the wall.

'Shall we say ladies first?' she asks, brow raised. I turn and walk towards the centre of the training pad. Everyone is staring. When I catch Harvey's eye, I see he is trying to give me a silent warning. Our easy communication does not always need words, and I can practically hear his voice in my ear saying, *Go easy on her; don't make a spectacle.*

I am going to have to work even harder if I am going to

pull off throwing this fight and make myself look weak to the other recruits.

I face my opponent. Today, Skai has her long hair pulled back in a tight ponytail, which makes the sharp angles of her cheekbones more prominent. She has the sort of defined beauty that girls my age envy. Her body is lean, yet toned. Still, I could tell that this was not going to be an even match.

'Now, I want this to be a fair fight,' Captain Wells addresses us, taking her time to look at us both in a silent warning, her eyes lingering on me the longest. 'This is not a knockout fight; there will be no eye gouging or hair pulling. I will ask one to be the offence, the other defence; then I will ask you to switch. This exercise is merely to ascertain your fighting techniques, so that I can determine what areas you need the most assistance in.' She then turns to the remainder of the group. 'As for the rest of you today, you can either practice sparring with your partners or you may practice independently on a bag. By the end of the morning, all of you will have undergone this assessment.' She turns her attention back towards Skai and me.

I watch as the others find their partners, and one by one, begin practicing their sparring. I watch as Harvey and Lewis move over towards a spare space where they could spar together. Ian storms off towards the punching bags; he begins wailing punches into one of the bags, clearly angry over being paired with Ren. I suppress a laugh.

I turn my attention towards Ren, who stalks over to the opposite end of the wall of punching bags, as far away from Ian as possible. I am anxious to see the result of their assessment.

'Mendez, you will be the offence in the first round, Foster, defence. After five minutes, I will blow my whistle and you will stop; you may have a short break if required, and then you will switch positions. Got it?' she asks, not really wanting to have to explain again.

'Yes Ma'am,' we reply in unison.

I looked over at Skai, nodding my head slightly to signal that I was ready.

Wells blows her whistle and calls, 'Begin.'

I take my stance, bracing both of my legs, readying for Skai to attack. She charges at me with a right hook that I immediately dodge by ducking, also missing her left fist as it tries and fails to connect with my face. Skai continues to throw punches at me that I block with my arms or by ducking. She is breathing heavily through her nostrils, not from exertion, but from frustration. I need to give her something. I am given the opportunity when she lashes out with her right leg in an attempt to knock me off of my feet. I dodge to the side to avoid connecting with the floor, but allow her to get past my guard.

She grabs my left arm and tries to pull me towards her to throw me off balance; I have to brace the impact on my legs, while blocking her right hook with my arm.

Skai grits her teeth out of frustration. I slam my elbow down on her arm that still has a hold of mine, making her hiss in pain and release my arm. I regain my ground and back away a few paces, bracing for her next attack. I can see her mind working, planning a new attack and I try to anticipate her next move, so that I can give her an opening.

She charges again, this time with a roundhouse kick, which I block with my arm, taking the brunt of the impact. Her left fist swings at my face, and I have to bend back to avoid the blow, while kicking out with my foot, which connects with her kneecap. Skai cries out in pain and falls backwards onto the floor.

The whistle blows and Captain Wells signals for us to stop. Our five minutes not yet over.

'Good. Mendez, you need to keep your guard up at all times, even when fighting offence. Other than that, you both did well,' she praises, as she writes on her clipboard. I take this time to memorise Skai's fighting techniques, or lack thereof. She always steps with her right foot before throwing a punch. She also hesitates before she swings, making me think that she is unsure of herself. That is her tell.

'Do you two need a break or are you fine to continue?'

I looked over at Skai. 'We can continue,' she says for both of us, breathing heavily.

'Very well, take your positions again, and when you are ready, I will blow the whistle again for you to begin.'

I take a deep breath and turn to face Skai again. Wells blows her whistle and it begins again.

I begin with a right hook, followed by a roundhouse kick that Skai easily dodges. I feign a left hook, which allows me to make quick jabs at her unguarded solar plexus. Skai growls with pain and attempts to block me, but is too slow. She changes her tactic and tries to knock my feet out from underneath me, while aiming a right hook to my chest.

I kick out at the knee that I had injured in our earlier fight; it buckles from both the shock of the impact and the pain. I take advantage while her balance is off and used my leg to swipe her feet out from under her, knocking her onto her back and onto the ground.

I walk over and use my foot to kick her in the chest as she is attempts to get back to her feet. I put my foot on her throat to keep her down, using just enough pressure on her airways, so that her vision begins to tunnel and she cannot fight me off.

Captain Wells sounds her whistle and barks, 'Foster, Enough. Release her.'

I remove my foot immediately and crouch down to check if she's okay.

'Are you all right?' I ask her.

'Fine,' she hisses, refusing any assistance as she slowly tries to get back on her feet.

Captain Wells eyes me suspiciously; she can tell I had gone easy on her.

I did try to listen to Harvey's warning; I held back as much as I could, but in the end, I couldn't contain my annoyance at the fact that they paired me with the only other female recruit, as if she could take me. If they really wanted to train us properly, then they would put me with someone who matched me equally. Skai was an adequate fighter and, given the proper training, she would improve. But I could not improve myself if I remained partnered with her. Surely, they could see that. I just hope that Harvey isn't mad that I ignored his warning.

'I think perhaps we may need to re-evaluate your pairing,' Captain Wells whispers to me quietly. 'For now,' she says at a higher decibel to both of us, 'take a rest if you need one. Otherwise, I would suggest that the two of you both move on to train independently—use the bags.'

Skai walks over to one of the benches and sits down. I make my way towards the punching bags, while Captain Wells calls over the next pair to spar.

The only remaining bag is the second from the end, next to Ren, who is watching my approach.

'What?' I ask.

'Nothing,' he says, the edge of his mouth turned up in a half-smile.

Again, I am struck by his appearance. He has a beautiful

heart-shaped face, and his full, pink lips draw my attention. This close, I can see the colour of his eyes; they are the colour of a storm cloud, a greyish-blue that I have never seen before.

'I couldn't help but notice how unevenly matched that fight was,' he says, and chuckles, his husky tone prominent.

'You noticed?' I ask dryly, though inwardly I was a little concerned. I had tried to hide my strength. However, if both Ren and Wells had caught it, I mustn't have been as subtle as I'd hoped.

He smiles, a full smile this time. 'It was hard not to notice a fight between two girls; I think everybody stopped to watch.' He chuckles again.

'Of course, they did.' I roll my eyes.

'Do you have a habit of making enemies wherever you go?'

'What do you mean?'

'I mean,' he says slowly, 'first Ian, then Chancellor Cain, now Skai. And we have only been here for twenty-four hours.'

'Firstly, that's only three people, and secondly, it is not like I intentionally went out of my way to make them hate me.'

'Well, for what it is worth, I doubt Skai will try anything anytime soon, now that she has experienced what it's like firsthand to be attacked by you, as for Ian, I wouldn't be surprised if he's stupid enough to try something. Best watch your back.'

'And what about you? How will you get them off of your back?'

'I can take care of myself,' he says slyly.

'I have no doubt that you can, but if you ever need a hand, I am here.'

He chuckles silently and turns his attention back to his punching bag.

'What city are you from?' I blurt out, my tone oddly flirtatious. *God.* What's wrong with me?

There's a long silence.

'This one,' he mumbles, before turning back towards his punching bag and ignoring me.

I watch him for a few moments; I can see the muscles move in his arms and his back with each movement. There's a certain kind of grace to his movements; his punches are quick and fluid—graceful.

I turn my attention towards my own punching bag, trying to process my thoughts with each punch I make.

'This one.'

Ren said that he was from this city, as in the military base. What did he mean by that? Was he born here on base, or was he trying to say that it didn't matter what city he was from before because this was now his home?

I would have to watch him, find out as much information as possible about him. I was curious to find out who he really was.

The rest of the afternoon was a blur of throwing punches at a bag and trying and failing to avoid staring at Ren.

When it was Harvey's turn to be assessed, I stopped to watch. Both he and Lewis were excellent fighters, but it was obvious that Harvey was better skilled. He was holding back. Something he never had to do when he trained with me.

I also stopped to watch Ian and Ren's assessment. Everybody in our entire group stopped to watch them have at it.

They were a blur of movements and an almost animal instinct took over them as they both became crazy with the bloodlust of the fight. Ian was far stronger than Ren, but he was so controlled by his rage that it was easy to see his weaknesses and his tell.

Ren was quicker, fast enough to keep himself at least two steps in front of Ian, which just angered Ian even further. It was like he was just toying with him, like he had the ability to end the fight at any time he wished, instead choosing to make Ian work for it.

Is that how I look when I fight?

When their assessment was over and both of them were bleeding from the injuries sustained, Ren caught my eye and smiled at me, knowing I had been watching him. He knew I had expected him to return victorious. I smiled faintly in return before turning back to my bag.

* * *

AFTER LUNCH, WE were ushered into one of the classrooms by Captain Wells for 'survival skills 101.' This training, along with our Genesi History training, would be the most valuable skills we could learn; anyone with common sense would tell you that knowing how to survive and keep yourself alive was vastly more important than learning how to fight or to shoot and kill. We were more likely to die from natural causes, such as the elements, starvation or infection than we were from a Genesi attack.

'In this classroom, you will be taught a series of survival skills that will become invaluable knowledge once you are deployed,' Captain Wells explained.

'I don't see how learning to kill a boar will help me kill any Genesi,' mutters Ian behind me.

I could hear a feminine chuckle from behind me. Skai.

'Could you please repeat your statement, Private Jenson?'

asks Captain Wells, her voice cool and authoritative.

'*I said*, I do not see how learning to kill a boar will help me to kill a Genesi.' Ian's voice is smug, as if he did not care for the consequences of talking back to our Captain. Perhaps he is not as intelligent as I assumed.

'The reason, and one you should do well to learn, Private Jenson, is so that if you do happen to come across any Genesi or are attacked by Genesi, you will not be half dead from starvation or delirious from dehydration. You are taught skills that will keep you alive, skills that will help you to survive when you run out of food and water from your packs or when you suffer an injury that needs treating and you have no first aid supplies or medicine. You are taught how to build a fire, so that you do not die of hypothermia during a cold night, and how to both build and find shelter to protect you from the elements. All of these skills you will need, and if you do not know how to keep yourself alive and to survive the most *basic* of things, how then do you expect to keep yourself alive when you are faced with a *trained* killer, Private Jenson?' Captain Wells was struggling to keep the annoyance from her voice as she reprimanded Ian. 'You will do well to pay attention during this training, Private Jenson, as it is clear you lack these skills right now.'

Ian did not speak for the remainder of our lesson. We spent the rest of the afternoon learning basic first aid. We learned how to correctly dress and bandage a wound, how to tie a sling, how to make a tourniquet, and how to provide CPR. We also learned how to read the signs of infection and how to identify various illnesses, diseases and infections. Harvey and I knew most of these already; we had spent years learning basic survival skills in the library back home and practicing on each other.

Captain Wells was impressed to see that we knew what we were doing already. Of all the people in our group, only three of us knew basic first aid: Harvey, myself, and Ren. I was amazed to discover that not a single other person in our group had bothered to learn basic first aid before applying for Delta Force, figuring they would be taught once they arrived. I did not expect to have the time to learn this, which is why I came prepared.

'You will all be required to take one of these tablets with you today. After each theory lesson, you will find the information of that lesson updated onto your tablets for you to read in your own time, and by the end of each module, you will be required to partake in an assessment. I recommend you utilise your spare time wisely. You may go,' she dismisses the class with a wave of her hand.

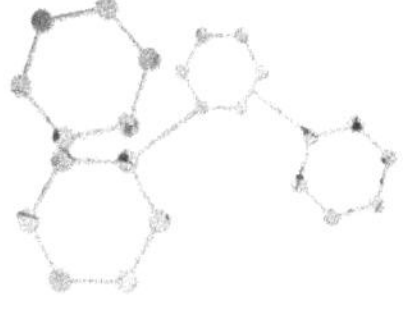

NINE

THAT EVENING, HARVEY and I found we had the entire dorm room to ourselves. The remainder of our dorm were unwinding in the rec room.

My mind wandered to Ren. I could picture him now in the rec room with a book in his hands, lips slightly parted in concentration.

I realised I was absentmindedly brushing a lock of my hair backwards and forwards along my lips, something I had done since I was a child when I was deep in thought.

I dropped the lock of hair that I had been holding and brushed my loose hair back behind my ears and out of reach. I needed to stop distracting myself with thoughts of Ren.

'I write and you talk?' Harvey asks, drawing my attention.

'Sure, where did you want me to start? Alphabetical or in preferential order?'

'Preferential order.'

'Okay then, let's start with Lewis,' I say. I watch as Harvey writes Lewis' name at the top of a blank page on the notepad he took from the rec room yesterday.

'Make sub-headings for computer skills, physical skills, behaviour and habits, hobbies, other skills,' I say, and wait patiently for Harvey to finish writing all of the subheadings I had listed off in his neat scrawl.

'Lewis has the particular computer skills we need; his physical skills need improvement, though, it is clear he was accepted for his intelligence with technology. I think he also struggles to make friends because he is a bit shy, but I think he is looking to you for a friend, Harvey.'

I wait for Harvey to finish writing down all Lewis' profiling; he says nothing to me as he writes, clearly not biting. I sigh.

'I really think he will help us, Harvey, if you become friends with him that is,' I urge.

'What makes you think he will help us?' he asks, none too nicely, as he looks up from the notepad in front of him. 'He told us the only reason he was here was to help out his family, to provide for them. He feels duty and honour bound to his family; I doubt he would go against that, even for us, Luka.'

'*Yes*, but I think that is where you are wrong. Lewis is driven by his duty and honour, that much is true, but something tells me he also feels that same sense of duty and honour towards our country because in keeping our country safe, his family will be safe. What better way to protect your family than by protecting your country, by usurping a corrupt country leader? What is more honour bound than that, Harvey?'

'I know you feel like we are just using him, and I know that you don't like it. You're a compassionate person, Harvey, and I *love* that about you. But it is what is going to get you killed. When the stakes are this high, you cannot show any compassion, Harvey, not even for me,' I say.

I know it's harsh, but it's the truth. Harvey's compassion was his Achilles heel.

There is a long silence as neither of us dares speak and I grow afraid that I have been too hard on him.

'Fine,' he says finally, 'who's next?'

I mentally breathe a sigh of relief.

'Ren Mason,' I answer as Harvey simply looks at me with his eyebrows raised, and a look of surprise.

'You cannot be serious,' he finally manages to say.

'I am serious,' I say, while watching him try, but fail to hide his annoyance, 'Harvey, did you see him today, in training when he sparred against Ian? You do not fight like that without proper military training.'

'What are you saying?' he asks.

'I'm saying I think he grew up on this military base. When I asked him earlier what city he was from, he was short with me and he started acting strange. Then, when he was sparring with Ian, it was obvious to me that he had had proper military training before, and he was the only other person besides us that already knew the basic first aid we were being taught today. *Don't you see it?* He must have grown up here. That's why nobody knew who he was when we arrived and why he did not want anybody knowing who he was or where he came from. He has already got the training; he knows this military base, we would not have to map out this facility if we had Ren as an ally.'

'Okay, say you're right...'

'I'm always right,' I interrupt, 'but go on.'

He sighs. 'Say you are right and he was raised on this base, that would mean he would have to have at least one parent that lives here on base permanently for that to happen. That parent would have to notice if he helped us, don't you think? Do you really want to risk that?' he asks.

I had already thought of that. Ren's mother or father would have to be pretty high in the military for their child to be born and raised here on base, which narrowed down the suspects significantly to only one. There was a reason why Ren had looked familiar to me, a reason why he tried so hard to keep his past a secret. There was no mistaking General Thorn's features in our new dorm mate. I should tell Harvey that I already know who Ren's father is, but for some reason, I can't. I never keep secrets from Harvey, but I know that if it were him, his moral compass would be telling him that it was not his secret to tell. So I do what Harvey would do if he were in my situation, I keep my mouth shut.

'I know,' I reply, 'but you will just have to trust me on this one.'

'Okay, I do trust you. I trust that you know what you are doing.'

I wait patiently for Harvey to finish writing down Ren's profile on the notepad.

'Anything else I should know about him?' he asks.

'Nothing that I can think of at the moment,' I answer instead, 'but we need to get close to him, find out what he knows about this facility and if he knows anything about my father. He may have met him when my father used to visit this base.'

'Okay, but I think that should be you. You would have a better chance at getting him to talk than I would; after all, he has not said one word to anybody since he got here, except to you.' He was looking at me seriously now. 'I doubt it will be long before others start to notice that too,' he adds.

He meant Ian.

'I'll get close to Ren if you get close to Lewis,' I challenge.

He hesitates for a moment as if weighing up the only option he had.

'Fine.' He sighs, defeated.

'Better add Ian Jenson to that list, as one to watch out for,' I added. 'He was clearly enlisted based on his physical capabilities, but he is no meathead. He has explosive anger issues and an almost animal instinct when he is in a fight, but he can't see clearly when he is in a rage. That's his biggest weakness. He has lived his whole life doing whatever it takes to keep himself alive... imagine him out on the field.'

'Yeah, I picked up on that too. Plus, I don't think he takes female authority seriously, not after the way that he spoke back to Wells today. I bet if we had a male captain, he would show more respect.'

'I'm sure she will put him in his place, he won't like it, but surely he has to realise that if he continues to speak that way to a commanding officer, he'll be punished.'

Harvey was biting his lip, something he did when he wanted to say something, but knew that he shouldn't.

'I'm worried about what happened yesterday morning,' he says eventually, 'I can't help but feel like he is going to try something to get back at you for challenging him.'

Typical Harvey, always trying to protect me, and always worrying over things that he can't control.

'I know. But I can handle myself. And besides, Ren is the one that actually needs to watch his back, after Ian lost in that fight with him and in front of everybody, he isn't going just to let that go.' This meant that I had to watch Ren's back now more than ever if I were going to recruit him as an ally.

'Something tells me that Ren can look after himself. If like you say, he was born and raised on this military base, then he can take care of himself, Luka.'

'Add Skai Mendez to that list,' I add. 'She will likely be Ian's second in command.'

I watch as he writes down Skai's name after Ian's profile.

'I am going to try to see if I can glean any information out of Captain Wells.'

'Do you think that's a good idea?' he asks me, knowing how pointless it is.

'It will be a risk, but one that I need to take. If Cain is behind my father's murder, then this is much more complicated than we thought. It won't be a matter of simply hacking into the computer system and searching for anything on my father. If he is behind it, then any files on my father would be restricted and highly classified and almost impossible to access.'

'And you really want to risk everything on the chance that Lewis, a kid and likely computer geek, will be able to hack into a highly classified military computer system.'

'Gee, you don't give him much credit, do you?' I asked sarcastically. 'I already know he can because he has already hacked the computer system here.' I say casually, waiting for him to bite.

'What do you mean?' he asks, taking the bait.

'When we saw him in the rec room playing that computer game, he was playing against another player, yet he was the only person on a computer. That would mean that he would have needed cyber access, right?' I ask.

'Yeah, so?'

'So, did you see any cables? Anything that looked like a cyber-connection in that room?'

'No, but that doesn't mean that he is hacking into anything. The cables might just be behind the wall or something,' he says. I give him a dubious look.

'Not likely, they would not be able to connect to all of those computers if it were behind the walls—the signal would not be strong enough. He hacked into the cyber here, Harvey, so, trust me, he knows how to hack into a restricted computer system.'

'So, how am I going to convince him to hack into a highly classified military computer system without telling him the truth about *why* we need him to?'

'Tell him the truth then.'

Harvey's mouth hangs open. He silently closes it again. 'You really trust him?'

'I do. Lewis can be trusted, Harvey.'

I hope.

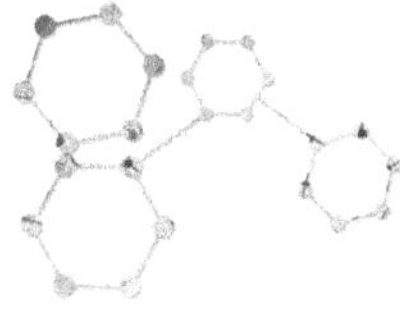

TEN

THE NEXT FEW weeks went by in a blur. In those weeks, I had not learned anything new in our training that I had not already learned back when Harvey and I were training at home. I didn't know how much longer I could keep up this ruse. Captain Wells was already too suspicious by how much I was holding back during training, which is probably why she changed my pairing to match me with Ren. Ian and Ren were unable to train together after that first fight, and according to Captain Wells, she believed that Ren and I would be more evenly matched, it did not go over well with Ian who had to be paired with Skai, as they were the only two left without partners.

But, at least, it gave me the opportunity I needed to get closer to Ren, even if I still had to hold back, at least, it was not by much. If nothing else, my re-match with Ren was more challenging than it was with Skai, and it earned me more respect from my peers. And, thanks to Harvey's pairing with Lewis, I have been lucky to gain his friendship.

Ren now sits with Harvey, Lewis and me in all of our theory training, and Harvey has been making great progress with Lewis. They spend their evenings together in the rec room playing online computer games, after Lewis showed Harvey how to hack into the mainframe and remotely access the cyber. It's nice to see Harvey making friends with somebody other than me. I have always felt that I was the reason that Harvey had no sense of normalcy in his life.

As for me, I spend my evenings holed up in the dorm room, alone. It's not so bad; I have the peace and quiet to concentrate on studying our training and committing it to memory, along with the map of the facility that I have drawn, thanks to Ren's help, along with all of the useful information that I have gathered on the people here. But, it isn't enough, I need to implement phase three of my plan, I need to get into the mainframe, I need to find more information about my father. I need more than my own thoughts and theories.

With a heavy sigh, I placed the notepad back under my mattress where I have been keeping it the last few weeks and slowly make my way from the dorm room, through the empty corridors and through the doors that led to the rec room.

The rec room is a buzz of noise and activity as I walk through the double doors. Like last time, the others were all busy watching the vision screens, playing games and video games.

I could see Ian and Skai by the same billiard table they were the last time I was here. This time, they are not playing, just talking. No, wait, they are flirting. *Gross.*

I turn my attention to the task at hand and begin to seek out the particular lounge chair I am searching for.

'Lookie lookie who finally came out to play,' hollers Ian as I walk past.

I ignore him and the sniggers and laughter that I hear from the others surrounding him. I keep walking until I find the lounge chair and the boy with messy dark hair and a book in his hands, staring at me.

'Don't look so surprised to see me,' I add dryly as I sit down in front of Ren.

He gives me one of his infamous half smiles, 'What brings you out of the dorm?' he asks me.

'Well,' I sigh, 'there is only so much theory you can commit to memory.'

'We both know that that's not all you are doing holed up in that dorm room.' He says frankly.

I look up at him then, he is staring directly at me, prompting me to be honest with him.

A test.

'You're right,' I reply casually, 'so tell me, what is it that you think I am doing?'

I wait for a response. He is silent for so long I almost hope that he is not going to answer.

'I think,' he says with deliberate slowness, 'I think that you are planning something, something big.'

'Wow,' I laugh. 'That could not have been any more vague. Real spot on,' I joke.

He chuckles, and at that moment, he looked young and vulnerable as if some of the walls he kept around himself were finally coming down.

'And what would you have preferred me say?' he asks me, 'That I see what you are doing, profiling the people here because you plan to sneak outside the wall and you need somebody to help you do it.'

I am not surprised by how observant he has been.

'But, it's not for some petty reason, is it? It has something to do with your father, perhaps who murdered him, and why?'

'Pretty much,' I would give away nothing.

He sobers then, hesitating before continuing, 'You may think that you are safe behind the walls you build around yourself, but sometimes, people can see through those walls, see the real you.'

I swallow. I hate feeling vulnerable.

'You're right, but that doesn't mean that you are safe behind the walls you build either, Ren,' I challenge.

He is taken aback, clearly surprised that I had figured him out so easily.

'How much do you know?' he asks in a whisper.

'Enough to figure out who your father is,' I answer softly.

'I see… I'll keep your secret if you keep mine?' He looks at me, his eyes pleading.

I am so consumed by Ren that I don't notice the group suddenly descending upon us until it's too late and they are right on top of us.

'Well, well, well, looks like the ice princess finally came out to play,' says Ian, smugly. He clearly thinks he is clever creating a nickname like that.

I stand to face him.

'And look,' he drawls, 'Prince Charming has come to her rescue.'

I turn to see that Ren had also stood at Ian's approach.

'What do you want, Ian?' I ask.

'What do I want? What do I want?' he repeats my question. I grit my teeth.

'Yes,' I reply, struggling to keep the frustration from my voice, 'What do you want, Ian?'

'I want to know what it is that the two of you are up to,' He responds, pointing between Ren and I.

'We aren't "up to" anything,' I grind back.

Ian chuckles. 'Yes, you are,' he says, 'you two think that you are so clever, but I see right through you. I know you both have been holding back in training, I know you have been reading up on your history.' This he says, directed at Ren. 'And I know that you aren't just studying when you are all alone in the dorm room,' he says to me. 'You two are hiding something, and I want to know what it is.' He steps dangerously close towards me, his face inches from mine. His breath stirring my hair.

'Sounds to me like you don't actually know anything,' Ren challenges, aggravating Ian further.

'I know that you grew up on this military base,' he threatens.

I look over at Ren out of the corner of my eye; I can see the muscles in his jaw tightening, he is going to give himself away if he is not careful.

'Looks like we are not the only ones hiding something, are we, Ian?' I challenge, in the hope to draw Ian's attention from Ren, it works.

'What's that supposed to mean?' he snaps back.

'I mean, you claim to be some Neanderthal that was accepted here purely for your strength in a fight, but it's more than that, isn't it?' I challenge, everyone is listening intently, waiting for me to continue. 'You have a near-photographic memory, something that is incredibly rare and makes you much smarter than you appear, and that is why you were accepted here.' It had the desired effect: Ian's face turns red with rage; he looks ready to boil over. 'You also have anger management issues, that much is clear,' I add.

'Why don't you prove it?' he spits. 'Or are you too focussed on solving Daddy's murder?'

My breath shoots out of me. White hot rage burns through me at the mention of my father, but before I can even move, Ren pushes past me and lunges himself at Ian.

Ian reacts immediately to the fight; he blocks Ren's punches and dodges his kicks. But, he is so busy defending himself that he is unable to land any punches himself, he was losing ground.

'Want me to tell everybody here who your father really is?'

he threatens, clearly trying to gain the upper hand. Ren waivers, giving Ian the opening he so desperately needs and he lunges himself at Ren, who is momentarily caught off guard.

Ian throws as much strength as he can behind his hits, lashing out at Ren. Ren's emotions are overwhelming him. He wouldn't be able to win this fight; I could see that. So could Ian.

I take a step forwards, meaning to interrupt the fight, but something has caught a hold of my wrist. I turn to see Harvey standing behind me, his eyes pleading.

'Let go of me,' I say through gritted teeth.

'Don't be stupid,' he hisses back, keeping his voice low. 'You could blow everything.'

'I know what I'm doing,' I grind back as I yank my wrist free and plunge into the fight.

By now, Ian has Ren on his back on the floor, he is landing hit after hit to Ren's face. Ren tries desperately to block the hits and protect his face. *It's now or never, Luka.*

I jump in and grab hold of Ian's fist as he is about to swing it at Ren's face again and drag him backwards, slamming his body onto the polished marble floor. As he tries to rise to his feet, I kick him in the chest, throwing him back to the ground, his head slamming against the floor with a sickening crack. I walk over and slam my boot into his face. I can hear the cartilage breaking in his nose from the impact of my boot. Ian is out cold. Blood begins to pool from his nose and onto the floor. My vision begins to show flashes of red as the rage inside me refuses to recede.

The room is silent, aside from Ren's ragged breathing until the doors fly open with a bang and Thorn comes striding into the room, a murderous look about him.

Thorn strides towards me, stopping a mere half-metre from me.

'You two,' he yells pointing towards Ren and I, his voice murderous, 'pick Jenson off the floor and follow me,' he turns on his heel and strides back the way he came. Just before he reaches the door, he turns back. 'NOW,' he yells.

With a quick glance at Ren, I rush forwards to pick up Ian's unconscious body. I have one arm slumped over my shoulder, Ren has the other arm, and together we drag Ian's unconscious body with us and follow the general.

Thorn leads us from the rec room, through the empty hallways, and up a flight of stairs. Dragging Ian up the stairs is the hardest part, and Ren nearly drops him at one point. We exit on the ground floor, and the general leads us down a hallway until he disappears through a doorway. We manage to drag Ian's body through the doorway and into the infirmary.

Thorn points towards an empty cot and we moved to place Ian down on the cot as a nurse appears to tend to him. I turn back to face Thorn.

'Follow me,' he says quietly as he walks from the room. I hastily followed him back out of the infirmary and into the hallway. He stops before a door and swipes his security access card before it opens silently.

I follow through the open door into what was some sort of conference room. There is a large round table in the centre with chairs set up around it. At each chair space, there are laptops placed for what I can only assume are for use during meetings. Without intending to, Thorn has just led me to the one room I have been searching for, a room that has computers that are able to access the mainframe. From one of these computers, I could hack into the restricted files. Or at least, Lewis could.

It's too easy.

Thorn turns and closes the door behind us.

'Explain yourselves.'

We look at each other, uncertain of what exactly we should say, or rather, how much of the truth we should say.

'I gave an order,' he shouts.

'Ian came over, he wanted to pick a fight,' Ren speaks softly.

'Did he now?' the general speaks sarcastically, he has stopped inches from Ren's face, 'And why would he want to pick a fight with *you*, what makes *you* so special?'

Ren swallows, he is nervous in front of his father, 'He threatened to out my heritage, Sir,' he says quietly. I had to strain to hear him.

I see the fear in Ren's eyes; he's afraid of his father, of what his father might do if he learns that others have figured out who Ren really is. I can picture Ren as a little boy, frightened of his father, scared of what he might do to him. I feel sick knowing that this is how Ren had to grow up.

'I see.' He moves away from Ren and comes to stand directly in front of me. 'And you, Private Foster, what is your involvement in this?'

I hesitate, not knowing how much I should say. Do I protect Ren or myself?

'As Private Mason said, Private Jenson threatened to... expose his heritage, and when it became clear that there would be no stopping him, Private Mason elected to keep him quiet by force. I thought it best to intervene to deflect suspicion away from Private Mason,' I answer, then hold my breath, waiting for reprimand.

'And you know of Private Mason's heritage?' he challenges.

'No, Sir, I do not. Though whatever it may be, I thought it best to be kept quiet.'

Whether he believed my lie or not, he does not say and

instead paces about the room for several heartbeats before he comes to a decision.

'Very well, Private Foster. However, the two of you have committed a serious breach of conduct. You will both receive non-judicial punishment for your insubordination as fighting among your fellow recruits is a punishable offence. At the end of each day, while your fellow recruits are off unwinding, the two of you will be completing a series of chores as part of your punishment. I will arrange for Captain Wells to oversee your punishment, as she is your ranking officer. You will show up each evening and complete the chores asked of you until she is satisfied that you two have learned your lesson on fighting your fellow recruits. *Is that clear*?' he asks.

'Yes, Sir,' we both answer.

'Private Foster, you may go.' He says, though not bothering to look at me when addressing me, his attention focussed purely on Ren.

'Yes, Sir,' I reply.

'Private Mason, you will stay a moment.'

'Yes, Sir.'

General Thorn looks over at me then, his eyes demanding that I leave the room.

As I make my leave, I look back at Ren; he has that frightened look in his eyes again, my heart aches for him. I don't want to leave him alone with his father.

I open the door and make sure to close it behind me. I take a few steps down the corridor and then backtrack as quietly as possible, placing my ear against the door to listen.

I can hear Thorn addressing Ren.

'Quite the mess you have made.'

'I am sorry, Sir.'

There is a muffled choking sound.

'I asked you to get close to the girl,' Thorn hisses. 'Your

foolishness has landed both of you at the centre of attention now. The exact *opposite* of what I asked of you.'

I can hear Ren struggling for breath. 'Sorry... Sir,' Ren rasps out.

'You had better find a way to fix this,' Thorn hisses. 'You need to find out why she is really here, but the girl cannot know that you are watching her.'

'Are you so sure that's why she is really here, Sir?' I could hear the timidness in Ren's voice as he spoke.

'I beg your pardon?'

Silence, then, 'Well, so far, I have not found anything unusual about her, nothing to suggest she is what you think she is and nothing to suggest that she is here because of an ulterior motive.'

There was another choking sound followed by a thump against the wall; I could picture General Thorn's hands around Ren's throat as he slams his head into the wall.

'You are not looking hard enough,' General Thorn hisses back as Ren's choking becomes stronger. 'Chancellor Cain suspects her and you will do well to follow his orders, or face the consequences,' he threatens.

I could hear Ren gasping for breath again.

No wonder Ren is so afraid of his father. It's obvious that Thorn has treated Ren this way since Ren was small. He must have been so frightened. Any anger I should have felt at the knowledge of Ren spying vanished, replaced by sorrow and pity.

'You may go,' Thorn continues. 'Oh, but one last thing: if I find out that she is aware that I am your father, rest assured, there are methods in which I can make her forget. Do not forget what I am capable of, Son.'

'Yes, Sir, I understand.'

'Good, now get out of my sight.'

He can make me forget?

I run as quietly as I can down the hallway, I had to make it back to the dorm room before Ren. Would he tell his father if he realises I had been listening?

I cannot get Thorn's words out of my head. He had said that he knew ways to make a person forget something. Was that what had happened to me the day my father died? Did somebody do something to me, to make me forget? Could it have been Thorn?

The moment I enter the dorm, Harvey leaps from his bunk and is already standing in front of me before I even finished walking into the room. The others are not back from the rec room yet, but I can see that Lewis and the twins are in the dorm already.

'What happened?' he asks anxiously.

I keep my voice as quiet as possible. 'We were let off with non-judicial punishment. We both have to report every evening with Captain Wells to do cleaning as punishment for fighting.'

'And where is Ian? What about him?'

'Ian is in the infirmary, and I am not sure whether he will be punished. Actually, I doubt he will.'

'What do you mean?'

'I can't talk about it here, but let's just say that the general has had me watched the entire time I have been here.'

'Come on,' he says annoyed. 'You have to give me more than that, Luka.'

'Sorry, but I can't. I'm not sure it's safe to talk anymore'

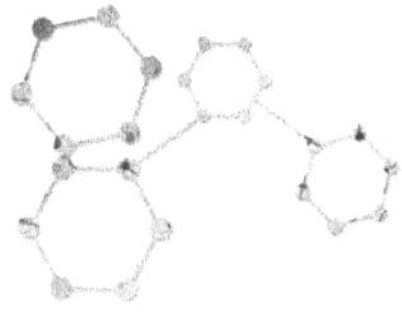

ELEVEN

'BEFORE I TELL you what your punishment is, I want to know what it was the two of you were thinking, fighting in front of everybody like that.' Captain Wells questions us the following evening, 'You do realise that the two of you are being watched.'

How the hell does she know?

'What do you mean we are being watched, Captain?' I ask innocently.

'I mean that General Thorn and Chancellor Cain have asked that the two of you should be watched. I have been told to report anything and everything back to them about your training, your behaviour, who you talk to—*everything*.'

'I don't understand, Captain, why are you telling us this?' I ask.

'Because,' she replies, 'I am trying to help the two of you survive here. You are both the top-ranking recruits, and I have had to lie and mark you down, to avoid suspicion from the other recruits and from the chancellor.'

I knew that she had noticed how much I was holding back during training. But why was she lying for me? And why was she lying for *Ren?*

'Luka, you already have a target on your back because of your father; the others would think that you are only being ranked so high because of your father, not because you truly are that skilled. And Ren, the same goes for you, the others are suspicious about you and where you come from, I know that you do not want that getting out. I have had to lie about both of your rankings and provide false reports back to General Thorn. Neither of you realise how dangerous it is for you to be here. Neither of you realise what they would do to you if they knew the truth.'

'We understand,' I say. Ren is either too dumfounded to find his voice or he was truly afraid. Truth was, I didn't really understand.

'I truly hope that you do, the two of you need to keep your heads down from now on. I can only protect you so much.'

'You don't need to protect us; we can take care of ourselves,' Ren grunts.

Wells glances over at Ren, and is silent for a long while before deciding to speak. 'No, you can't, not by yourselves. Get cleaning those guns; I will be back in on the hour to check on you. I suggest you get started and make it look like you take this punishment seriously.' She doesn't wait for our reply as she turns and walks from the training room, leaving me alone with Ren.

I walk over and sit down on one of the two stools that are provided. There is a pile of guns that we are required to dismantle, clean and put back together again. I begin dismantling the first gun, while Ren stands behind me frozen, watching. It seems as though he is planning to say something to me, but in the next moment, he comes and sits down on the other stool and picks up a gun.

We worked in silence for over half an hour. If I don't speak now, I will lose any chance to speak to Ren in private. It was now or never. I take a breath to steady myself.

'I overheard your conversation with your father last night,' I say, my voice loud in the otherwise silent room. I glance at him to gauge his reaction, but he does not give anything away.

He was quiet for a long while before he answers. 'How much did you hear?' he finally asks.

'All of it,' I glance over again to gauge his reaction. He has now busied himself with dismantling the gun on his lap, so I can't see his features. His control is slipping. I just have to push a little further.

'Why did you lie to your father?' I ask curiously, prompting him.

He sighs and puts down the gun. 'I lied to protect you.'

'Why?'

'Because for some reason, my father and the chancellor seem to think that you are a Genesi or at least part Genesi. *Why?* I have no idea. I'm protecting you so that you don't end up as some sick sort of experiment for them.' He struggles to keep the disgust from his voice. This was not the response I was expecting and I am at a loss for words.

Eventually, I find some words. 'That still doesn't explain why you protected me, though. Why you chose to protect me over yourself.' My voice stutters, still overwhelmed.

'Because,' he sighs again, 'I don't want you to end up as one of their experiments, and because you and your friend are going to end up getting yourselves killed if you get caught. You will end up just like Sam.'

Alarm bells start ringing in my head. *He knows what really happened to the chancellor's son.*

'You know what happened to him?'

'Not the truth, but I've seen enough of what goes on here to know what would have happened to him.'

'What would have happened to him?' I dare ask.

He sighs. 'Before he was deployed outside the wall—I'm talking six months before—he disappeared for a while. And, when he returned, he didn't remember who I was. Didn't remember much of anything. That was my father and Cain's doing. And if you are not careful, you will end up getting caught just like Sam.'

'Getting caught?' I could feel all the blood draining from my face.

'Don't think that I am the only one who is suspicious of you being here,' he says, as I continue to stare at him, unable to hide my shock. 'Everyone was suspicious when they heard that Luka Foster, *the great scientist's daughter* was coming to join Delta Force.'

I swallow to hide my discomfort in talking about my father. My stomach felt as though it was filled with rocks.

'You're not here because you want to get into Delta Force; you're here to finish whatever it was that your father started.

I am at a loss for words.

'I want to come with you,' he says suddenly.

'Come with me *where*?'

'When you leave to find the Genesi. That's what your planning, isn't it?'

'No, absolutely not.'

'Why not?' he challenges.

'Well, for starters, how can I be sure I can trust you? You're supposed to be spying on me for your father, so how do I know that you do not just want to come along, so that you can report back to him.' I challenge

'You *don't* know,' he retorts, 'at least not for certain, but you trust me, anyway, don't you?'

'What makes you so sure that I trust you?'

'Because you're not afraid of me, you're afraid *for* me,' he answers slowly, 'I see the way you have been looking at me today, full of pity like I'm some sick puppy that has been kicked to the curb. You would not be looking at me that way if you didn't think I was innocent. I really wish you wouldn't look at me that way, though.'

'Well, you're not innocent, are you? But, you're right, I do trust you, and I have no idea why.'

I couldn't pinpoint exactly why I believed that he was trustworthy, but I knew for certain that he would not betray me.

'Why do you want to come with us?' I ask instead.

He hesitates; I could see the uncertainty in his eyes as he argued with himself whether or not it would be safe to tell me.

'Look,' he says, 'I don't care what it is you plan to do or how you plan to do it, I will help you every step of the way, I will give you all the answers that I know. But, when it's done, I want to be left alone, free to live outside and on my own.'

He was looking at me, waiting to read my reaction, whatever it may be.

'You want to live outside the wall, alone?'

'Yes.'

'*Why?*'

'Because I would be free. I would be safe from my father and no longer his puppet.' His voice is reserved.

'How long has your father been abusing you?' I whisper, dreading his answer.

He couldn't meet my gaze. Instead, his eyes lingered on the floor.

'I was told that he wasn't always like this, that he was not always so cold and cruel,' he whispers.

'And what changed him?' I whisper back.

'My... mother. She died giving birth to me.'

'And you think that he blames you for her death, is that it?'

'I don't think it, *I know it,*' he says bitterly.

My heart ached for him, for that little boy that grew up without a mother and instead with a father who blamed his existence for his mother's death. I reached over and placed my hand over his.

'It's not your fault, don't *ever* believe that. Her death may have been a part of what changed him, but the corruption was caused by somebody else, somebody who thrives on manipulating people when they are vulnerable.'

'What are you implying?'

'I am implying that I think Cain got to him, corrupted him, and that that is what changed him.'

He clears his throat. 'What can I do to help you and your friend?'

I let the subject drop. Clearly talking about his father was hard for him, something else we had in common.

'Do you by any chance know how I could get back into that conference room undetected?' I held my breath.

'No,' he whispers, 'But, it you give me some time, I am sure that I can find a way.' He grins at me. I grin back.

We are interrupted as Captain Wells walks back into the room, our hour up.

* * *

A WEEK PASSES, and in that time, Ren has shared with me everything that he knows regarding my father, Thorn and Cain during our nightly cleaning duties. Ren has helped with profiling for potential others and taught me the layout of this facility. Everything he knows he has shared with me, but I have not had the chance to share it with Harvey.

Tonight, we are tasked with cleaning the mess hall after dinner. Captain Wells had again left us for the hour, and I had busied myself with wiping down the tables when I felt Ren standing right behind me, I spun to face him.

'I know how to get into the conference room,' he mentions casually as he picks up a cloth and begins helping me wipe down the tables.

'Really, how?' I struggle to keep the excitement from my voice.

I watch as he reaches into his pocket and produces a small white rectangle.

'This swipe card should get you into any area of this facility. It's a master one.'

How on earth did he manage to get that?

'Okay, but where did you get it?'

Please don't let it belong to his father.

'Don't worry, it's not my father's,' he says as I breathe a sigh of relief. 'Well, it's his spare that I swiped before our first day.'

Panic fills me.

'Don't worry, he has never used it before, so there is no chance he will notice it missing. I thought I might need it one day, so I stashed it somewhere for safekeeping. I had trouble finding time to go back and get it,' he admitted.

'If you have a master security card, then why are you still here? Why didn't you just leave like you wanted to?' I ask.

'Because,' he hesitates, unable to meet my eyes, 'when I was planning my escape, I heard that you had applied, I overheard my father and the chancellor talking about it and I wanted to find out why they thought you were so important.'

'And did you? Find out why I was important, that is.' I tasted bile in my throat.

'All I found out was that they are convinced that your father did manage to re-develop the Genesi code, and that he used his only sample on you. At least that is their theory; they can't be certain if it is true. Nothing substantial was detected in your blood, so they don't exactly have any proof.'

I swallow. Without realising it, he has just confirmed my theories. Cain thought I was Genesi.

The man is insane.

'I already guessed that that was what they thought I was. I need to find out exactly what they are planning, and as much information about it as possible. I need to be prepared.'

'Then we better do this soon.'

'Tonight, we go tonight.'

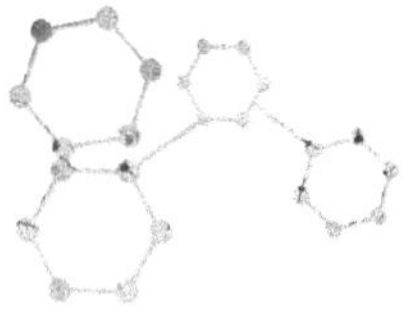

TWELVE

I HAVE NO idea how Ren managed it. While I was busy quickly getting Harvey up to date with our plans, Ren was somehow able to convince Lewis to help us in under five minutes.

Harvey had spent weeks buddying up to Lewis, so that he could convince him to help us. But Ren just walked over and asked him. Just like that. I felt like a fool.

I had long ago trained my body to wake at a set time, that way, if I ever found myself without an alarm, my body had its own inner alarm system. I woke at 0100 hours and checked to make sure everyone in the dorm was fast asleep before I crept over to the others and woke them one by one. By the time I got to Ren's bed, he was already awake, and we simply stood there staring at each other until Harvey came and nudged my elbow, rousing me from thoughts and signalling to me that it was time to move.

After checking again to be sure that everyone in the dorm was still soundly asleep, we slipped out of the room as silently as possible, ensuring the door closed soundlessly behind us as we crept down the dark and deserted hallway.

We made our way soundlessly down the hallway until we reached the door for the stairwell, Ren stopping to swipe the security card to allow us access to the stairwell. We climb up one flight of stairs and come out into yet another sleeping hallway, this one leading to the conference room.

When we reach the door to the conference room, we all have to stop again for Ren to swipe his security card. I wince at the clicking sound it makes when it accepts the card and the door clicks open. I quickly scan both ends of the hallway to ensure they are still empty. I walk into the room first to check that the coast is clear; the others follow me once I give the signal, and soon we were all inside the room with the door locked behind us. I am able to breathe again.

'I'll guard the door, you just do what you have to do, Luka,' whispers Ren as he moves to stand behind the door so he could listen out for any sounds from the hallway, angling his body so that he can still watch us.

'Thanks,' I say quietly to Ren, 'Lewis, are you sure you still want to do this?'

Lewis' voice is hoarse from sleep. 'Well, it's a bit late now to back out. I'll be fine, just as long as you take the blame if we get caught,' he jokes.

He often jokes when he was nervous or uncomfortable. I watch as Lewis walks over to the first available laptop and sits down. He powers it up and the darkened room is bathed in an eerie glow as the screen lights up.

'It's password protected,' he grumbles to himself.

'Do you think you can get past it?' I ask nervously, it's now or never, after all.

'Of course, I can.'

I let loose a breath I didn't realise I had been holding.

'Don't forget that I am the only one here who is a computer geek,' he jokes, but it falls on deaf ears. No one is in the mood for jokes.

The room fills with the sound of his fingers moving hastily over the keys on the keyboard in a flourish of tasks and commands. The computer screen is now black with bright green numbers and letters drifting across the screen.

With each keystroke, I become more anxious that he might not be able to crack the encrypted password.

'And we are in.'

I breathe out a sigh of relief. 'Can you get us into the mainframe, and then after that, into the classified section? We are searching for restricted files.'

'Yeah, that's already done, I mean I figured that that's what you wanted me to do.'

Wow, he's fast. Next time, I won't doubt him.

'Thanks, Lewis, could you please search Christopher Foster, my father? I need to know what they have on him.'

'Sure,' there was another flourish of keystrokes.

I turn to check on Ren. He is still standing guard by the door. He smiles at me encouragingly and I cannot help but smile back at him, something about the way that he smiles always has me undone.

'So far, there isn't much on your father,' Lewis comments, drawing my attention away from Ren. 'I would assume it is possible that anything about your father might be kept on a personal computer, and without knowing whose computer or the details of the computer, I won't be able to hack it.'

I try to hide my disappointment. 'That's okay, I understand. What did you find, anyway?'

'Well, there's this video file,' he clinked onto the file and the screen becomes filled with an image of my father. He is sitting on the chair in his study. He looks so real; I could already hear the way he would sound in this video. I have already watched it a thousand times, but seeing his face like this is making me remember all the little things about him that time is threatening to make me forget.

'I recognise this video,' I breathe, 'this is the video that my father left for me the night before he died.'

'You mean the one that had been tampered with?' Harvey asks as he walks over to get a closer look at the screen.

'Yes, that one. But I don't know how anyone here managed to get their hands on it. It was left on his personal computer, for me, and it was password protected.'

'It's possible they pulled it from your father's computer after he died, back when they were investigating his death. And it would have been easy for somebody like me to find their way past the password protection,' Says Lewis.

'We should watch it,' Harvey breaks in, 'I have a feeling this copy has not been tampered with. And, whatever is on there, it must be important. Otherwise, they wouldn't have it. And I bet that whoever got this copy of the video from your father's computer is also the one who tampered with the copy that you have.'

'Okay.' I try my best to sound brave. 'Play the video,' I command, voice wavering.

I watch Lewis hit 'enter' on the keyboard, and I soon become filled with the feeling of déjà vu when I hear my father's voice speak the words that I have heard him say a thousand times over, words I have long since memorised.

'*Luka, as you already know...*' I listened to the same speech again, but this time there was more, I was sure of it.

'*Now, Luka, I need you to pay very close attention to what I am about to tell you. What I am about to say is going to change everything...*'

'Pause it,' I demand; I can barely breathe. My chest is beginning to feel tight. The anxiety cannot attack me now. I beg for it to stop.

'Are you okay?' Harvey asks me, concern ringing in his voice.

No, how could I be?

My heart is racing with the anxiety over finally being able to hear the rest of the message that my father had intended for me all those years ago. My palms are becoming sweaty and I am having trouble keeping my breathing quiet. The others must have noticed by now, but don't comment on it.

Harvey comes to stand beside me. I feel his hand reach for mine and I hold on. His fingers squeeze mine to reassure me that he is right here beside me, I squeeze back to tell him I appreciate him being here with me. He would always be my anchor.

It's time to be brave, Luka, time to finally listen to what your father has to say, even though it scares you, even though hearing the truth is going to break your heart, you have to be brave.

Be brave.

'You can press "play",' I say to Lewis, barely hearing him press 'enter' on the keyboard again.

'*As I said before, long ago, before you were born, I began working on the Genesi Project. It started with developing a cure, but then it became much, much more than that. When you were born, you were different. The blood test they administered on you as a newborn showed that you had a mutated gene. Your DNA was unique to what I had ever come across before and what has been recorded in history. It was more evolved than any other human DNA I had ever seen and I am not proud of admitting this to you, but I studied you, I studied your DNA.*

'*Because of your DNA, I was able to find the breakthrough I so desperately needed for the development of the cure. The senate wanted my discovery kept quiet; they told me that they had to run further testing before they could release this development to the public's knowledge.*

'*That was when Chancellor Cain approached me with a proposition. He wanted me to work for him and develop a second generation of the Genesi Code, a Genesi Code 2.0, so to speak. But he wanted to make some changes to it; he wanted to be able to control the subjects rather than giving them their free will. He wanted genetically modified human soldiers at his disposal, following his will.*

'Naturally, I refused; I told him that I wanted no part in his experiment. That is when he threatened you and your mother. He told me he would have you both killed if I did not cooperate. I don't need to explain the details to you, but I'm sure you can understand how convincing he was.

'With no choice left but to cooperate, I began working on his experiment. I used your evolved DNA to help me reproduce the second generation of the Genesi code.

'But, instead of informing Chancellor Cain of my finished work, I lied and kept it a secret. I told him countless times that it was not quite finished or that it still needed more testing before it was ready. I lied because I could not let him have it. I needed time to find a solution out of this mess, a solution that kept both you and your mother alive.

'Over time, Cain became suspicious, that was when he sent General Thorn to investigate.

General Thorn started asking questions, he suspected the truth and I knew that it was only a matter of time before he reported his suspicious on to Chancellor Cain. I became desperate.

'Luka, I am not proud of what I did, but please, understand that I had to hide my work somewhere, so that one day if it ever was needed, you could help finish this war. I had to find a way to ensure that both you and your mother survived my mistakes. I know you are smart enough to figure that I am not referring to a geographical location. I will not say anything more in case somebody else discovers this video and it leads to the wrong hands, I cannot let anything happen to you, you are everything to me, darling.

'I have taken to destroying all of my research and all of my work, so that Cain can never destroy what is left of this world.

'When you are old enough to understand what he is capable of, I hope that you can understand why I did what I did, and why I am asking you to finish what I started.

'Luka, you need to find the Genesi. They are not dangerous like we have been led to believe. After each generation, the Genesi Coding that is inside them has become diluted. They are scarcely even Genesi anymore. They are more closely related to humans than to the Genesi. Chancellor Cain knows this, but he does not care. He has wasted years of valuable research and resources on developing a cure that was never needed, instead of using that knowledge and resources on rebuilding our nation; he wasted it to fund his thirst for power.

'He believes that if he can rid our nation of the Genesi, society will see him as their saviour. He believes that by keeping everyone in fear of the Genesi, he will remain in control. Society has a right to know that these people are no longer a threat. That they should be welcomed back into our society and cared for. They are human beings, no matter their DNA.

'Luka, you need to find a way to finish this war. Chancellor Cain has proven that he is more than capable of taking innocent lives, and that's just what he will do. He will kill thousands of innocent lives to secure his power and only you can stop him.

'You know how to cure them, Luka; the cure is in your blood. It always has been.

'Be strong, Luka, be brave, I know that you have it in you to be the true saviour of the human race. Remember that I love you, no matter what happens to me, I will always love you.'

The video cuts to black abruptly; the room is silent. My heart feels like it's breaking with the absolute devastation of hearing the truth, it is almost too much to bear. Tears threatened to fill my eyes and I struggle to keep them at bay.

It's been almost a decade since I have cried, does my body even know how to cry anymore? Isn't crying a human emotion? Am I even human? All these thoughts float through my otherwise silent mind.

I cannot face the others; I cannot even look at Harvey, even though I know that he was looking at me. I could not bear to see the pity written across their faces and I know that I cannot hold back the tears if I did look at him.

I try to steady my breathing, so that my voice does not break when I finally speak, 'Lewis, could you please search my name?'

His voice wavers a fraction, 'are you sure you want to do that?'

'Just do it,' I breathe, my voice wavers.

Now, the only sound in the room comes from Lewis' fingers, typing away commands in order to achieve the desired result. I am grateful for the silence as I try, but fail to steady myself.

'Do you want me to read it out loud, or would you prefer to read it by yourself in private? We don't have to know what's in your file. I can copy the file for you so that you can read it in private.'

'No,' I sigh, 'It's okay. We all heard what my father said, we all need to know the truth,' I feel Harvey give my hand another reassuring squeeze. I do not squeeze back this time. The muscles in my body are no longer functioning properly.

Lewis clears his throat, 'There's...umm...a fair amount on you, they have copies of all your school files, reports and test results, they have a copy of your application for here and your aptitude testing, and...umm....they have a copy of your blood results and DNA reporting from when you were born. The report that is with it says that your DNA is unique, evolved... something about a mutated gene. They also have blood results from the recent sample that was acquired when you applied here. The report says that your DNA strands appear similar to a Genesi, but also appears identical to human DNA at the same time. It goes on to mention that they think you may be some sort of Genesi, human hybrid of sorts, but that they can't be sure as they have never encountered anything like your DNA before.' He turns in his chair to look at me. 'Do you want me to continue with this?'

I clear my throat and take a measured breath, 'I need to hear the truth. Whatever it may be'

He nods at me and continues reading.

'Okay, the next file goes on to report on your father's... murder. Says that you were found unconscious that day by a friend, and that you have no memory whatsoever of what happened. It says that you were the one to discover your father's... body and that is the first thing that you remember that day.'

He turns to look at me again. 'Wow, Luka, I'm so sorry.'

'Please... just continue reading.' My eyes begin to burn.

'Umm... it also says that during the ongoing investigation, you were asked if you had ever met Chancellor Cain and General Thorn, and that you do not recall ever having met either of them previously.'

'Wait, stop,' Harvey and Lewis both turn to look at me.

'What? What is it?' Harvey asks.

I hesitate, 'Harvey, before we received our acceptance letters, do you recall me ever telling you if I had met or seen Chancellor Cain or General Thorn before? Think back as far as you can. Try to remember.'

He is silent as he searched his memory, 'No. I can only recall you ever telling me that your father was working for the chancellor, and that he would often come to this base to meet with him, but that's it. You have never told me before if you have met either of them. I think the first time that I know you met Chancellor Cain was when he handed you your acceptance letter because I don't remember you ever meeting him or General Thorn at your father's funeral. Because you refused to attend. So, you couldn't possibly have met them before. Could you?'

'That's what I thought,' the others were clearly confused. 'As far as I am concerned, I had never met either of them until that day when we received our acceptance letters. So, then why does that report sound like I have met them before and just don't remember it? There is only *one* day missing from my memories.'

'You think that you met them the day that your father died, and that you don't remember it?' Harvey asks, sceptical.

'That's exactly what I am thinking.'

'It is possible?' Ren speaks for the first time, 'I mean, you heard what my...I mean what General Thorn said last time we were in this room, that he knows ways of making a person forget. Maybe you did meet them that day, or see them; maybe he made you forget.'

'So you're saying that Chancellor Cain and General Thorn most likely killed her father and then did something to Luka to remove her memory of it happening?' Harvey asks sceptically.

'Yes, that is what I am saying. According to your father, they both seem to have no concern over killing innocent people.'

'Is there anything else on my file?'

'Nothing much, but there are some reports from Captain Wells addressed to General Thorn, looks like she is just providing reports on your training. But wait...'

'What?' we all ask.

'Well, it's wrong. She says that you struggle to keep up

with training and that you are average among the recruits, but that's not true, not even close. Why would she lie about that?'

'Because she is protecting me. She told me that General Thorn had asked her to report on my training, and she told me that she has been lying about it.'

'But why would she protect you?' Harvey asks.

'Because she knew your father,' says Ren.

'She did?' I ask, unable to hide the hurt from my voice. *Why didn't they tell me this before?*

'Yes, she would have met him every time he came here to visit General Thorn or Chancellor Cain. They would have run into each other at some stage. I think she knows more than what we think she does,' he says.

She knew my father and never told me.

'What are you going to do, after tonight I mean? Are you going to leave and find the Genesi like your father told you to?' asks Lewis.

I deliberate for a long moment.

'Yes, I am going to do what my father asked me to do. But this has become so much more than finding my father's killer. I need time to think. I need to adjust my plan.'

'What time is it?' Ren asks suddenly.

'According to the computer, it's 1:37 am,' Lewis answers promptly.

'We need to get back,' he warns.

'Okay, Lewis, log off the computer, and make it quick,' I tell him quickly.

We waited patiently while Lewis copies all the information onto a memory chip that Ren had obtained. He then backtracks through the computer deleting any evidence of us being here before he logs off and turns off the computer, putting it back exactly as it was when we came in.

We all followed Ren from the room and back to the still sleeping dorm room. I crept back into my bed and listened for hours to the others breathing until I am sure they have all fallen asleep. There would be no sleeping for me tonight, not after everything I had just learned

I lay in bed, processing all of the information from tonight, committing it all to memory. The memory chip, tucked safely away inside my sock—where it would remain with me at all times until I had the chance to look at it again.

First, my father had experimented on me. His video confirmed what I have always feared, that he hid his only sample of the second generation Genesi coding inside me and most likely my mother too.

Second, my father had developed some sort of cure, which Chancellor Cain had covered up. I can recreate this cure as the key is hidden somewhere in my blood. But is it still there with the Genesi coding running through my veins?

Chancellor Cain blackmailed my father into developing the second generation of the Genesi coding, one that would control the person infected with it. That led me to believe that Chancellor Cain was planning some sort of army. Why else would he need a second version of the Genesi code?

Third, all of the signs pointed towards Chancellor Cain and General Thorn being behind my father's murder. They probably had him killed to keep him quiet. But, although Chancellor Cain would have commissioned the kill, General Thorn would have been the one to pull the trigger. Then they both covered it up.

Fourth, it was no longer safe for me to be inside this facility. I need to leave. I have to do as my father asked; I have to find the Genesi.

This suddenly has become more than avenging my father. Thanks to my father's eye-opening video, this has become a war. I am probably the only person capable of stopping it. Only I don't know how I am supposed to stop a war. Yet.

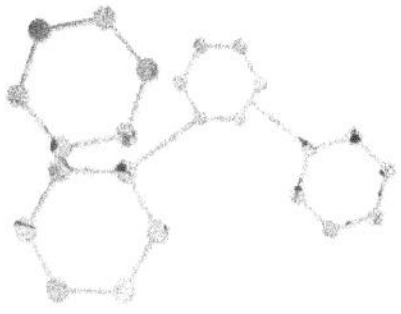

THIRTEEN

THE FOLLOWING EVENING, Harvey, Ren and I are all standing in the dorm room after dinner. The others from our dorm are in the rec room enjoying their free time.

Ren was standing behind the door, ready to block it in case anybody tries to walk into the room and stumbles into our conversation. Earlier this evening when we were fulfilling our punishment, I filled Ren in on my plan, and we were able to work on it together.

'I guess you have a plan,' Harvey says sceptically.

'I do,' I retort. 'It's not the best plan given what little time I have had to make it, but it's better than nothing.'

'Well, let's hear it,' he nods for me to elaborate.

Suddenly, Ren's body becomes completely rigid and he braces his full weight against the door. The door is suddenly pushed from the outside and I watch as Ren places even more of his strength into keeping the door closed. I should have been able to hear someone approaching, if I had been paying attention. I should have been paying more attention.

'Guys, it's me,' a muffled voice calls from the other side of the door. 'It's Lewis. I swear, I'm here by myself. I just wanna help.'

Ren and I exchange a quick glance before I nod for him to let Lewis into the room. He opens the door slowly; I can see the muscles in his back tense, readying himself in case there is somebody else on the other side of the door with Lewis.

Lewis is standing in the doorway, looking awkward and uncomfortable, and completely alone.

'Well, hurry up then,' Ren barks as Lewis scurries past him.

'What are you doing here, Lewis?' I ask.

'I umm... I wanted to join you.'

'Join us?' I question.

'I want to come with you when you go. I want to help stop this war.'

I loose a heavy breath. 'Lewis, do you know what you are asking?'

'Probably not,' he blushes, 'but I saw that video too, Luka, I know that it's not safe here. I know that Cain is corrupt and I am smart enough to figure that they are planning to start a war, and that they are probably going to use us recruits for their army. I would rather die for your cause than for his. I know I won't be that useful, but I want to help in any way that I can.'

The boys are silent as I process Lewis' request.

'I don't want anybody to die on my behalf.' I swallow the lump forming in my throat. 'Are you sure you know what you are signing up for? Once we leave these walls, we will be known as deserters. Are you sure you want that?'

'I am.'

'Very well, you can join us. Right now, we are planning our way out of here. Think you can help with that?'

'Sure.' He nods enthusiastically.

'Good, now we need to find a way out of this facility. We need to gather supplies to take with us, and we need to find some form of transportation once we are outside the walls. Otherwise, they will surely catch us.'

'Do you know where the Genesi are?' asks Lewis, 'do you know where it is we have to go?'

'Not yet,' I hesitate, 'but I am sure that I can figure it out. It's in my DNA after all.'

* * *

THE NEXT MORNING in training, while we are practicing our hand-to-hand combat, General Thorn walks into the room, followed by the male officer who was our to guide on our first day.

I watch as General Thorn pulls Captain Wells aside and leads her from the room. The male officer remaining behind to oversee the rest of our training, or rather, to oversee me. I catch his gaze lingering on me.

I turn to Ren, Harvey and Lewis, and nod my head in the direction of the back wall where the punching bags are lined up. They nod their understanding.

'Don't look at me when we talk; I am pretty sure we are being watched by that male officer. Just act casual and keep your attention on the bag in front of you,' I murmur.

Ren immediately catches my meaning and begins practicing basic manoeuvres into his bag; I follow his example.

'Can you think of a reason why Thorn wants to speak to Wells in private?' I ask, keeping my voice down. I throw a couple of punches into my bag while I wait for a response.

'There could be a few reasons, but my gut is telling me that he knows,' Ren whispers to the group.

'That's what my gut is telling me too, do you think she will cover for us? Or do you think she will rat us out?' I ask.

'I am not sure; I don't really see how much she could really tell anyway, she never saw us—nobody did—so, I don't see how exactly they know or can prove anything.'

'Either way, we need to make sure we have our story straight,' whispers Harvey.

It feels like an eternity when General Thorn reappears. However, Captain Wells is not with him. He stands before our unit and calls us to attention.

'Private Foster, Private Mason, Private Montgomery and Private Kingston, would you kindly follow me,' he calls and my stomach fills with lead.

Crap.

He leads us back to the conference room, my stomach in a state of dread the entire walk. As we enter the conference room, General Thorn makes sure to close and lock the door behind us.

'Take a seat,' he says to us, while gesturing to the round table. I walk over to the table and take a seat, while the others follow soon after. General Thorn comes to sit directly opposite me. I try my best to keep my features composed. I cannot show any emotion in front of the general.

'Do you know why I have asked you here?' he asks no one in particular.

'No, Sir,' we answer together.

He smirks, 'Very well then, two nights ago, somebody broke into this very room and accessed our restricted computer system. You two,' he says, while pointing towards Ren and I, 'were the only ones among the recruits who knew that this room existed. So, I am going to ask you once more, do you know why you are here?' his voice laced with threats.

'No, Sir,' we say together.

'Well then, let me tell you my theory,' he leans forwards from across the table, 'I think that after learning this room exists, you two managed to swipe a security card to gain access to this room again. You roped Kingston here into helping you access the computer network. And I dare say that Montgomery tagged along because he follows you everywhere like some love-sick puppy,' he spits.

His theory was more than just a theory and he knew it, but he had no proof, that much was certain.

My knuckles clench reflexively under the desk. 'Where is Captain Wells?' I ask instead.

General Thorn smirks at my question; it distorts his features, making him look twisted and cruel like a savage dog.

'Captain Wells is being questioned back in the main facility.'

'I don't understand, Sir; you are accusing us of something we did not commit, yet Captain Wells is being questioned for it as well. What could she possibly have to do with any of this?'

'Captain Wells is responsible for the lot of you. If you fail, she fails. If I can prove that you are guilty, she will be equally punished for failing her duty,' he was almost smiling now.

'But she didn't do anything,' I say, 'and neither did we.'

'Awfully defensive for someone claiming to be innocent.'

'Or maybe I am defensive about being accused of something I did not do. My entire future is on the line, after all,' I snap back.

'I am afraid it is much, much more than just your future that is on the line, Private Foster,' he threatens as he rises from his chair. 'The four of you will wait here a moment, while I retrieve Chancellor Cain who has just arrived on base and escort him to the main facility. You will then be escorted to the main facility and will be questioned individually by myself and Chancellor Cain, and I can be *very* persuasive. You will not be able to leave this room, it will be locked upon my exit, and there will be guards posted outside, in case you attempt to escape,' he threatens as he walks from the room, the door clicking as it locks behind him.

'Shit, what are we going to do now?' Lewis asks, unable to keep from panicking, his voice raising several octaves.

'Nothing,' I mutter.

'Nothing?' his voice rising even further.

'Yes, *nothing*. We are going to go along with his requests and be questioned. He has no proof to back up his theory. Although come to think of it, how could he possibly have known that someone logged into the system, I thought you erased any trace of us being here.'

'I did,' he says defensively, 'there is no way anyone would be able to know I was in the system, I ghosted.'

'Okay,' I say slowly, while trying to come up with a plan, 'Then how does he know that someone was in the system?' I ask.

I look to the others, but none of them have any good answers.

Ren slaps his hand down on the table, making us all jump. 'The security card, it would have registered being used. Dammit. He must have known that I had taken it, and he never said anything because he wanted to trap me into using it and getting caught. I am so sorry, this is all my fault.'

'It's okay, Ren; it's going to be okay,' I say, placing my hand over his to reassure him.

'Then what do we do? What's the plan, Luka?' Harvey asks, an edge to his voice that I had never heard before.

'I'm thinking, okay.' I was struggling to keep the panic out of my voice. I had to keep a controlled front, so that the boys did not panic. I had to remain calm, even though my heart was hammering in my chest. If I fail, they fail. And my father fails.

We couldn't sneak out of the room, sure, we could take the guards posted outside the room, but the swipe card was back at the dorm. There was no way that we could unlock this door, which meant that we had no choice but to go along and be taken to the main facility, and questioned individually. Unless we were able to break away once we were led out of the room.

A moment later, noises sound outside the door; I could clearly hear the sound of a struggle, the scraping of boots along the floor. Then a loud thud, followed by another. In the blink of an eye, the door clicks open and Captain Wells steps through the door.

'If you want to get out of here, you have to follow my orders, and we need to hurry.'

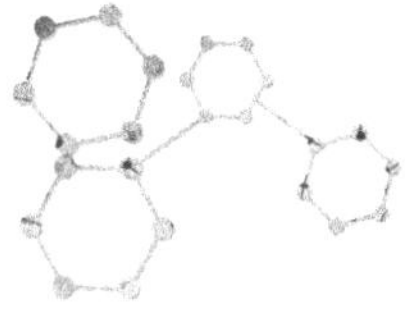

FOURTEEN

'CAPTAIN WELLS?' I ask, astonished, 'What are you *doing* here?'

'Rescuing you bunch of morons, of course,' calls an all-to-familiar voice as Ian steps through the doorway. He is still dressed in his training clothes, but he holds a gun in his hands. I notice that Captain Wells is also dressed in her training clothes, but has on a grenade belt and multiple guns and knives strapped to her bodice. She is dressed for battle.

'I don't understand,' Lewis declares, shaking his head.

'You don't have to,' Captain Wells is saying. 'But we have to go *now* if we all want to live. We have about two minutes before anyone realises that I am missing, so that gives us approximately three minutes to get out of here, hopefully longer if my diversion works.'

We did not need to be told twice. We scramble from our chairs to follow Wells and Ian from the conference room. I watch as Ren stopes to quickly unplug the chords from the laptop in front of him, yanking at the chords until it comes free. He shoves it into Lewis' hands before leaving the room with a look that tells Lewis to hold on to that laptop as if his life depended on it, which is true, of course. I watch Lewis nod in understanding.

As I step through the doorway and into the hall, there are two bodies on the floor in front of the conference room. They had to have been the guards that General Thorn warned would be posted outside the room. Now they lay crumpled on the floor, unconscious, but alive. Skai is standing over the two guards; her gun pointed between them in case one of them rouses. She is still dressed in her training clothes and the look on her face is grim but determined. I am surprised to see her.

I smile weakly at her as I bend down and pick up the gun from the body closest to me. The male officer's hand twitches when I pull the gun from his hands, but thankfully, he does not wake. I then grab both of the daggers from his belt. When I stand, Ren has already picked up the other gun from the second guard.

Wells throws Harvey one of the handguns that she had strapped to her, that way, we each have a weapon, except for Lewis who holds the laptop in his hands.

'We had better hurry,' Wells says, nodding down the hall. 'This way, follow me.' She begins jogging down the empty hallway.

The others immediately follow suit, jogging down the hall after the captain, I make sure to go last, so that I can cover us from behind. I keep my ears trained on any sound of pursuit.

We don't get far, the others have stopped before a set of large double doors, the doors that lead from the training facility to the hallway that connects to the airport, I remember. We are going to the airport. The doors slide open with a whoosh and the others begin jogging through the now open doors, and into the long hallway, I follow at the rear.

I look over my shoulder every few seconds, checking if we were being pursued. So far, there is nobody following us, and as we are not slowing down in any way, I can only assume that we had not come across anybody up front either. *Something is off.*

By now, someone should have noticed us. At the very least, Thorn should have been back by now with the chancellor and they should have noticed the unconscious guards and the empty room. Wells said she had about two minutes before anyone noticed that she was missing, but, by my estimate, it has been two points three minutes already, which means that any second from now, we will have people hunting us.

We must have reached the end of the hallway as the others have all stopped again. I stop too and make sure to check behind us, even though I know we are not being pursued; I would have heard them already if we were. I can't help but feel a sense of unease. *Something is definitely not right.*

The set of double doors open under Wells' request, and we all scurry through the doors to stand in the foyer of the airport. I aim my gun, ready to shoot at any threat. But again, there are none. Nobody is here; it is deserted. *What is going on?*

'Something is wrong,' I say quietly, to no none in particular. 'There's nobody here and we weren't followed. Surely, someone should have noticed us all by now.'

'I set off a diversion,' says Captain Wells, 'One big enough to buy us enough time to escape, well, *hopefully* enough time. They should be here soon. Come on, this way,' she says, as she heads for the hangar doors. I don't have time to wonder what kind of diversion as a sudden loud screeching noise blasts through the airport's foyer. An alarm.

Crap.

We all run.

As I enter the airport hangar, I notice immediately what the diversion is. The force field is down. I cannot see its shimmery ripples overhead. That would explain why we are headed for a hovercraft, because the force field is down, that meant that we could escape by air. That was also a big enough dilemma to cause enough panic to deter the attention away from all of us. It was brilliant and I could not help but admire Captain Wells. However, she had managed it. *She must have had this planned for a while.* The alarm that had triggered was because of the force field being down, not because of us. Still, I do not let my guard down.

We run for the closest hovercraft, there are approximately ten or so in the hangar, but we only needed one.

Just then, my ears pick up the sound of footsteps behind me. I whirl around just as someone yells out. 'Hey stop!'

I aim my gun at a young man who appears to have been on duty guarding the hangar. I hear the door to the hovercraft descending, but, despite the distraction, I hold my gun steady, pointed at his head. He swallows. I can see the panic in his eyes.

'I said stop,' says the officer, his voice wavers just a fraction. He is unarmed and has a gun pointed to his forehead. I raise my eyebrows at him and he raises both hands in the air, a sign of his defeat. I keep my gun steady, not trusting the soldier.

'Captain Wells, you can't do this—you can't leave,' he says. 'They will know it was you and they will come after you. You will not survive this, you will be killed without mercy for your treason,' the officer pleads to Captain Wells, voice still wavering. He appears around the same age as Wells.

I look back at Captain Wells; if she's worried about what the male officer had said, she doesn't show it. She just turns around and boards the hovercraft.

'What do you want to do with him?' Ren yells over his shoulder, the alarm still sounding.

'Take him with us,' I say, making up my mind. Ren looks at me horror struck, and I explain. 'We can't leave him for anyone to find and we can't shoot him—the sound will cause unwanted attention, even over this alarm. The best solution is to bring him with us; we have no choice.' With this, I raise my right hand holding the gun and slam the butt of it into the officer's skull, knocking him unconscious. I haul his unconscious body up the ramp of the hovercraft.

I drag his heavy body over to an available seat and Harvey helps me to lift the officer into it. I strap his body in and push his head back to inspect the blow I landed on his skull. It has already swollen and is beginning to bruise. I hope I made the right decision sparing him and bringing him with us.

I can hear Wells instructing Lewis to use the laptop in his hands to scramble our flight plan, so that we can't be tracked. Lewis nods as he walks over to a seat and begins strapping himself in.

'You know how to fly this thing, right?' I ask Wells as she turns to look at me.

'It's been a while, but I'll manage,' she says to me, 'It will be a little bumpy, so you all need to strap yourselves in,' she calls to the rest of us as she moves for the cockpit to take a seat in the pilot's chair. I can hear the hum and feel the vibration of the craft as she starts flicking switches to power up the craft.

I walk over to the empty chair next to Harvey and begin strapping myself in. I am seated between Harvey and Ren. Then between Ren and Lewis is the unconscious male officer. Lewis has the laptop turned on and is already hastily typing in commands, the keystrokes drowned out by the hum of the engine.

I hear the first gunshot hit the outside of the hovercraft.

Shit.

The hovercraft slowly and shakily begins to rise, causing a feeling of vertigo to go through my body. My heartbeat begins to race and I can feel my pulse beating in my ears. *God, I really hate flying.*

A second gunshot sounds. Followed by an entire round of shots. Then it stops abruptly.

We continue to slowly rise into the air, and just like Wells warned, it is a little bumpy. I know that I am not the only one who feels like vomiting. Both of my ears pop, causing that uncomfortable feeling in my ears like last time and my hearing becomes muffled. Thankfully, it does not last long and my heartbeat begins to slow as Wells announces that we have cleared the range of the force field and have reached the right altitude. I still feel incredibly nauseated.

I look over at Harvey; he is bouncing his right leg up and down like he always does when he is anxious. I reach over and place my hand on his knee, pushing down slightly to make the bouncing stop. He looks over at me.

'That's not helping,' I say quietly.

'Sorry,' he mutters.

We are all silent until Wells announces that we have now cleared the base and are flying over open land with no sign of pursuit. *But, what about the shooter, where is he?*

Several minutes pass, then thirty. Wells confirms that there is no sign of pursuit.

Now that we are safe, for now at least, I decide to speak up.

'Does anybody else think that was too easy?' I have to yell over the hum of the engine to be heard.

'Yes,' Ian calls back, 'but it's a long story,' he is seated directly across from me, and for probably the first time in his life, he looks nervous.

'Well, you best start at the beginning then,' I call back.

'Nuh uh, you're going first, princess,' he calls back.

'Good thing we have a long flight ahead of us,' calls Harvey. 'We may as well pass the time by getting each other up to speed with things. One of you better talk first.'

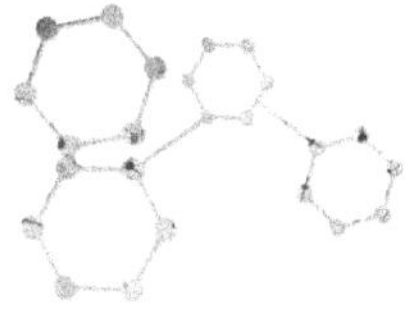

FIFTEEN

'I'LL GO FIRST,' says Ren, uncertainty ringing in his voice.

No, please, don't.

I try to catch his gaze, my eyes pleading him to reconsider. He cannot tell them the truth about who he is; they'll hate him for it—Ian especially. He reads the look in my eyes and shakes his head lightly.

'I'll go first,' he repeats, this time sounding sure of himself.

Everybody is looking at him now, Ian staring smugly, he had been waiting for the day for Ren to admit who he really was. Well, now it was finally here. And it's all my fault.

Ren exhales heavily and clears his throat. 'My father... my father is General Thorn.' He waits for the news of this to sink in.

I hear Harvey's intake of breath immediately, followed by Skai's loud gasp. Even Lewis stops moving, his hands hovering over the keyboard, but too shocked to continue typing.

'I knew it!' Ian cries victoriously.

I can't help but roll my eyes. *What a prick.*

'I knew there was something off with you. Now, it all makes sense.'

'Would you just shut up, Ian?' I yell.

I cannot bring myself to look Harvey in the eyes, I know how betrayed he must feel, how disappointed in me he will be once he realises that I have known this entire time. Out of the corner of my eye, I can see the gears working in his head as he processes, putting it all together.

'How long have you known?' he whispers to me.

Damn, he had to ask.

I take a deep breath to steady myself and tell him the truth. 'Since the first day.'

'And you never told me,' he accuses, struggling to keep his voice quiet and even.

'Oh look out, lovers' quarrel,' Ian hollers across the craft, smirking at me.

God, I would love to punch that smirk off of his face.

'Shut up, Ian,' I say through clenched teeth, trying hard to control my rage. 'Ren, how about you finish your side of the story, *explain*,' I say, none too kindly.

'Right,' he says, 'before I got accepted into training for Delta Force, Chancellor Cain came to see my father and I. They both told me about...' he hesitates, glancing at me with uncertainty.

'It's okay,' I whisper, nodding my head for him to continue.

He clears his throat. 'They both told me about... Christopher Foster's daughter, and how she had applied for the Delta Force training. They wanted me to keep an eye on her, observe her and report back to them.'

I could see how tightly Harvey's jaw was clenched, his knuckles whitening as he clenched his fists.

'You mean spy on her,' he spits.

'Relax,' I whisper to him, 'it's okay, I already knew about it.' He looks at me, hurt written in his countenance. Yet another thing I kept it hidden from him.

'So you were sent here to spy for Daddy?' Ian growls.

'Yes,' Ren deadpans.

'So how can we trust you?' he asks.

'The same way we can trust you,' I say to Ian, 'because you are here. Because you escaped with us. Since we have no choice. Which option would you prefer? We are now all deserters; I think that speaks for something. Tell us your side of the story.' I direct the conversation back to Ian to take some of the heat off of Ren.

All arrogance washes from his face.

'Well...' he hesitates. 'It all started when I realised who Daddy's boy here was,' he gestures to Ren. 'When Thorn came to visit me in the infirmary, he asked me a lot of questions, questions about you,' he says, looking at me.

I swallow. 'What did you tell him?'

He scoffs. 'Not much. I may hate you, but I hate him more. The man gives me the creeps. He wanted to know what you were like, in training, outside training, who you spend your time with, that sort of thing. I mostly said that I hadn't taken much notice. Which is of course, a lie. But, it got me thinking, about what you and your lover boy were up to.' At this, he nods towards Harvey. 'I saw how differently Captain Wells treated you; I saw how everyone treated you, it was as if they were afraid, not of you, of course, but of what you might do, because of who you were. At first, I thought you were here to investigate your father's murder, but I know now that it's about more than that. This is about finishing whatever it is that your father was murdered for.'

He looks at me seriously now, all the mocking gone from his voice. 'When Captain Wells was taken into questioning and you lot were led away by the general, I knew that something was wrong. So naturally, I had Skai here fake an injury to her leg, so that I could have an excuse to take her to the infirmary and look for you lot instead. As we were headed to the infirmary, Captain Wells burst into the hall looking like a total badass that had just escaped from hell.

We both realised'—he nods at Skai, who hasn't said a word the entire time and was currently looking at her feet—'that something was about to go down and that we could either be a part of it or not. Captain Wells gave us the choice to leave now and go back the way we came or to follow her, so we followed her.' He shrugs as if it were nothing.

'Wells explained that she had set up a diversion but that we needed to get the four of you out first—she can explain the diversion later. That led us to the two guards stationed outside your door. Wells and I knocked them out. I'm sure you remember things from there.'

'Okay, I guess once we stop, Captain Wells needs to tell us what the hell happened.'

'Yeah, now come on, ice princess. I spilled my guts, your turn,' Ian challenges.

I hesitate a moment, ticking off in my head what I should and what I should not tell. I know that I had to tell them most of it, but there are a few things that I'm going to keep to myself, things that they don't need to know yet. Things I'm not ready to talk about yet—like the memories that have been flashing through my mind since I saw the rest of my father's video. Every time I try to reach out and grab a hold of a memory, it slips away.

I look over at the male officer; he has been silent the entire time, so quiet I almost forgot that I brought him along. He is awake, and he is staring back at me, clearly waiting to hear what I have to say. I swallow.

I start at the beginning, with the day I woke up to find my father had been murdered. I explain how Harvey and I had spent the better part of a decade preparing for finding the man who had killed my father. And, I explain what we had learned since coming here, about Chancellor Cain and General Thorn, about the video of my father, and about where my father hid the sample of his formula, finishing when I reached the part where we were rescued by Captain Wells and Ian. Nobody speaks as I tell my story, and after I finish, nobody speaks for a very long time.

'Makes sense,' Ian says finally. I expected some smart-arse remark from him, so I am surprised at how calm he is.

'What does?' I ask.

'You.'

I stare at him, confused, but he does not elaborate.

We spend the rest of the flight in silence. The overall mood is pretty low, considering that we are now considered deserters. We have all deserted our duties and escaped outside the wall. We would all be wanted criminals now, even the male officer. He had not said a word the entire flight. I watch as he listens intently whenever anybody speaks. I figure once we land, he might try to escape; however, there won't really be anywhere for him to escape to. Hopefully, he will understand what it is we are trying to achieve, what it is we are deserting for. I hope he chooses to help us; we need all the help that we can get. But, if he chooses to fight us, I may have to kill him. I am not sure that I am ready for that.

I pass the time by processing the information from Ian, which is not much, but it is better than doing nothing. I need to hear Captain Wells' side of things, how she escaped from the main facility, how she had managed to disable the force field. I can't stop thinking about how easy it was when we escaped; it was too easy. *Something is not right.*

'Oh no,' says Lewis, voice ringing with panic.

'What?' I yell.

'Umm guys... there's another craft headed our way.'

I unbuckle myself quickly and make my way over to Lewis. My legs are unsteady from the movements of the craft and I almost collapse on top of Ian who scowls at me and shoves me away. When I get to Lewis, I peer over his shoulder to get a better look at the laptop. There are two dots on the screen. One is our craft; the second is gaining on us dramatically. I run to the cockpit to inform Captain Wells.

'There's another craft gaining on us fast,' I yell over the noise of the engine.

'Shit,' she yells over her shoulder. 'Get back in your seat and hang on, it's going to get rough.'

I run back to my seat and strap myself in, right before the craft suddenly lurches to the left.

'They keep trying to gain access to our craft's computer system,' Lewis calls frantically, 'I'm blocking them, but whoever it is, they are good.'

'Can you stop them?' I ask, half yelling.

'I said they're good,' he yells over the noise, 'but I am better.' He begins frantically punching commands into the computer. Ren leans over to shoulder the computer steady for Lewis as the crafts continues to lurch from side to side.

'Lewis, does this hovercraft have any guns or cannons? Something to shoot another craft down?' I ask, an idea forming in my mind.

'Yeah,' he yells, not looking up from his computer. 'I can access the gun system from here. Wait, are you saying you want me to shoot them down?' he looks up from his computer, face stricken.

'Yes,' Ian, Ren and I call back.

'But what if I kill them? They could be innocent people, just following orders.'

I watch in horror as Ian raises his gun to Lewis's head.

'Shoot them down, or I will shoot you down.'

I am unable to move; I can't leave my seat without risking being thrown around the craft. Lewis is terrified and I feel guilty at being unable to do anything.

'Please,' he begs, 'don't make me do this.'

'Do it or *I* will,' Ian spits.

'Ian, put the gun down. We can find another way to get rid of them,' calls Harvey.

Ian positions his gun to aim directly at Harvey. Without a thought, my hands move to unbuckle my harness, but they are stopped as another hand grabs my wrist.

'Harvey, let me go.'

'No, he's not going to shoot me.'

'You wanna bet?' Ian says with ice in his voice.

'It's okay guys; I-I'll do it.' With a resigned sigh and trembling fingers, Lewis starts typing commands on the computer again

I can faintly hear the impact of the guns on the other craft but there is no mistaking the loud explosion that follows.

'They're gone,' Lewis whispers, his voice barely audible over the noise of the craft. 'I killed them I just… *killed* them.'

'It was them or us. Suck it up,' Ian shoots back.

I grab Harvey's hand to comfort him as Lewis begins to cry silently. My heart aches for him. I wish there had been another way. The cabin lapses into silence again.

'We're almost out of fuel,' comes Captain Wells' voice over the intercom. 'We'll have to land and walk the rest of the way.'

My spirits lift, as does those around me. Finally, we could get to the ground.

I watch around me as everyone sits up straighter, alert.

As we begin our decent, I feel both of my ears pop again, readjusting to the decline in altitude. *I am not going to miss this feeling.*

As the hovercraft touches down, we begin unbuckling

our seat belts. I stand up to stretch my legs; it feels so good to move my muscles and to stretch after sitting for so long. Harvey goes and checks on Lewis.

Wells exits the cockpit and comes to stand in the isle between us all. 'You can ask questions later. Right now, we need to gather as many supplies as we can from here and we need to set out on foot. We need to ditch the craft and cover as much ground as possible. Lewis has blocked them from tracking the craft, but soon, they should be able to find it using the satellites, or they will track the craft that was shot down. Once they find it, it will only be a matter of time before they are here and looking for us, so we need to get moving *now*.'

'What supplies do we have on board?' I ask, taking control of the situation.

'All crafts carry basic supplies in case of emergency landing. There should be plenty of food and water for a few days at least, first aid supplies, and some radios to signal for help, which we could use to monitor their communication. We better search the craft for anything else that might prove useful.'

We set out gathering the supplies; even the male officer helps, he locates where all the food and water packs are stored, along with backpacks that we can use to carry all of the supplies. I learned that his name is Winston, though he never said if that was his first or last name. And I didn't care to ask.

Once we had packed as many supplies as we could carry, we set out on foot, abandoning the craft.

Once we disembark, it takes a while for my eyesight to adjust. It is night already, but it is brighter than usual. Back at home, the night sky is drowned out by city lights. Here, the moon shines brighter than I have ever seen it and the stars are so bright, like a million tiny moons across the navy blue sky. It is breathtaking.

I can't see much scenery; I can only see approximately fifteen metres in front of me. This is enough to gather that we are somewhere where the land had been destroyed by the war. There are no landmarks, no buildings, no trees or shrubs, nothing but open land, which is either dirt, sand, or rocks. The Genesi would not be here; there is nothing for them to use to survive. There is nothing for us to use to survive.

'We need to cover as much ground as possible tonight. We will stop just before midnight and rest for a few hours, but then we will need to set out again at first light. Does everybody understand?' she asks, and we all nod in agreement.

'If my memory serves me right,' Wells continues, 'there should be a small town a few hours walk from here. We should be able to rest for a few hours in that town and then head underground to the rail tunnels that are underneath the town and continue from there.'

'You mean the rail tunnels that the Genesi live in?' Lewis asks nervously.

'The Genesi do not live in the tunnels, that is false reporting. It took me years to figure that out and find out where they are really hiding.'

'Where are they hiding?' asks Skai, speaking for the first time.

'The mountains, a few-days walk from here.'

'Captain Wells, while we are walking, it would be a good opportunity for you to tell us all how much you know,' I say casually.

She purses her lips, deciding whether or not to tell us. Finally, she yields. 'Very well then. Let's start walking and I will tell you everything I know.'

We start heading north, following Wells. The ground is uneven beneath my feet and my footfalls stir up dirt as I walk.

'We need to cover our tracks,' I say, searching desperately for anything useful to cover our footsteps only to come up short. I make a quick assessment.

'Everyone, form a line. Only step in the footprints of the person in front of you. *Do not* deviate from their tracks. We need to leave only one set of tracks.' If we were to all share the one set of footprints, people are less likely to assume it's a bunch of deserters, and more likely assume it's a rogue Genesi.

I don't need to tell them twice. They scramble to form a line with Captain Wells at the front and me right behind her.

'I will start at the beginning... I knew your father, Luka,' she says as she looks over her shoulder at me. Her voice is loud enough so the others can still hear— it carries through the night. 'I met him several times over the years when he came to visit the base. The last time your father visited was about a month before he died. He was acting strangely; he did not seem his usual self, he was drawn and dishevelled when I last saw him. I remember asking him if he was all right, and he snapped. He began ranting about how everything was corrupt, how Chancellor Cain was evil and how he knew that the Genesi were no longer a threat, but wanted it kept hidden from us all. None of it made any sense at the time. He kept telling me how sorry he was, over and over, but he would not tell me what it was that he was sorry for.

'General Thorn walked in on us and he took your father away. General Thorn never said a word to me after about what that was all about; it was as if he was pretending that it never happened. A month later, I heard about how your father had been murdered and I started to put some things together. I knew that it was not a coincidence that he had been killed. So, I began paying more attention to General Thorn, Chancellor Cain, and the senate. Your father had said that Chancellor Cain knew that the Genesi were no longer a threat, but when your father died, Chancellor Cain announced to the whole nation how your father was the only scientist ever to come close to developing a cure and how his loss would set us back.

'I knew that something was amiss. Chancellor Cain and General Thorn had been sending more and more troops outside the wall to hunt the Genesi since your father's death. If he knew that they did not need a cure, why then did he send out his troops? If he knew that no scientist would be able to develop a cure, why send out troops to kill them? Why not just bomb them all? Something was being covered up. I spent years trying to get to the bottom of it. And then I heard that you had applied for the Delta Force training, Luka. I knew straight away that you did not want to be a soldier and serve our country. I knew that it was about your father, and I knew that if I had realised this, then so had Chancellor Cain and General Thorn.

'They both came to me, told me that I was to be the one to oversee your training and that they wanted me to report to them everything about you. That was when I began to monitor you, for my own purposes, not theirs. You were... different to what I expected. At first, I thought it was due to how hard you must have trained before you came to the base, but then you really started to stand out from the others and I knew that it was something more, that there was something about you that *was* different. I had my theories. So, I made precautions if anything were to happen, I wanted to have an escape plan.'

'What kind of escape plan?' I ask, 'How did we escape?'

'A buddy of mine works in maintaining and repairing the wards for the force field. I asked him to set up a sort of safeguard so that if I needed to, I could temporarily disable the force field and escape. The safeguard would emit a virus into the mainframe, causing it to melt down, along with the entire computer system, including the monitoring cameras and speakers. This would distract everybody into trying to repair it as quickly as possible. I knew that General Thorn would be called to oversee the problem and that that would be enough of a distraction for us to just slip out.

'By the time that they would have gotten the computer system working again, it would warn them that the force field was down, but by this time, it would be too late, and we would already be gone. If we had been any longer than what we were, there was every chance that he would have caught us. He would have known something was wrong right away and would have gone looking for us. I would imagine we would have been just a few moments ahead of him.

'Anyway, that is basically what happened today when we escaped. When I was left in a room after being questioned, I used the computer in the room to enter the fail-safe commands that caused the system meltdown; this allowed me to escape from there and come to find you. By now, they would have gotten the systems working again and would know what transpired. They are clearly already trying to track us. They would have sent dozens of hovercrafts out after us. That's why we need to hurry; we can't let them catch up to us.'

'But if he was moments behind us, would he not have caught up to us by now? Something does not feel right.' I add

'He let us go.'

'What do you mean he let us go? Why would he do that?' I could not hide the anxiety from my voice.

'Because, he thinks you are heading towards the Genesi, which you are by the way. I would imagine he is hoping that you will lead him to the Genesi encampment.'

'Will we lead him to the Genesi encampment?'

'No, he still thinks that the Genesi are holed up hiding in the tunnels out here, he has no idea that they are in the mountains. If we can make it to the rail tunnels, then we should be safe. He won't dare attack the Genesi until he can gather enough forces, and by that time, we will have long cleared out of the tunnels.'

'So,' I ask, 'do you know exactly where we are?'

'We are a few-hours flight north of the base. The mountains we are heading towards are in the province that was known as Canada, before the war that is.'

Canada.

'And what exactly are we supposed to do once we do find them?' asks Ian.

Wells smiles, 'We follow Luka's orders, of course, since I am no longer captain.'

Ian chokes. 'No, Screw that?' he yells, 'I am not following orders from icc princess!'

'You are if you want to stay alive,' she yells back in response, not bothering to turn to facc him.

'Yeah right,' he is still yelling, 'she would be more than happy to see me dead.'

I sigh. 'Just *shut up* for once, Ian,' I struggle to keep snapping at him.

'Look,' says Wells. 'This is Luka's mission; it's all to do with her, to do with what she really is. So, she is the leader of this unit, and if you do not like it, then you can be left behind,' she threatens.

I expected Ian to say that he would rather be left behind, but he keeps his mouth shut. So does the male officer.

We spend the next few hours walking in silence. As the sky becomes darker, it becomes more and more difficult to navigate our surroundings. The moon and the stars are still our only source of light, as we had agreed not to waste the batteries in our flashlights, knowing we would need them once we reach the rail tunnels. Wells would use hers every now and then to check that we were still heading in the right direction.

The terrain we walk on remains a desolate wasteland. There is still nothing in sight besides more dirt and rocks. Occasionally, we come across a shrub, but they appear to always be on the brink of death.

After a few more hours of walking, I can faintly see shapes in the distance. *A town.*

The closer we get, the more I am sure that it is a town.

'Captain Wells?' I ask.

'Please, call me Liz, I am no longer your captain, and you are no longer a soldier,' she says quietly.

'Okay, Liz, do you know if that town up ahead is the town that we are looking for?' I ask pointing towards the shapes in the distance.

'I can't see any town yet, but your eyesight is far better than mine. It should be the town, judging from the time we left the hovercraft.'

'Do you think it will be safe for us to walk in to?'

'I'm not sure, I can't imagine anything being able to live out here, which makes me think that it's an abandoned town from before the war, but we had better be on guard and check it first, if it's clear that there are no signs of life, then I suggest we stop there for the night. The Genesi would not risk being on the surface.'

I could hear sighs of relief from some of the others at the mention of stopping for the night.

'Then it's decided,' I say to the others, 'we will inspect the town first if it's all clear, then we will stop for the night. But, if we see any signs of trouble, we leave, *immediately.*'

Everyone nods their understanding of the plan as we approach the town.

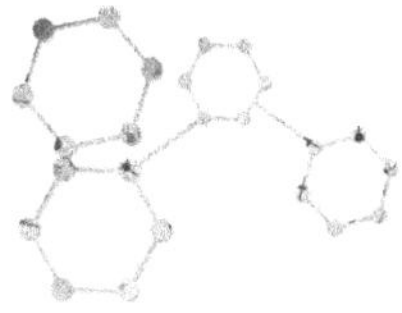

SIXTEEN

AS WE ENTER the town, it becomes clear that it has not been impacted from the waves of bombings from the war. No, this ghost town is caused by centuries worth of rust and decay. The main road is only just discernible under the dirt, sand and weeds that have colonised it. The homes and stores are clustered close together down the single main road, their windows shattered from the weakness of their decaying structure. Rotting weatherboards that have lost almost all of their paint and ceilings that had mostly all caved in on their dwellings, this I saw clearly despite the lack of daylight.

I switch on my flashlight to illuminate what I assume was once a store. Inside, I can see shelves that are bare, aside from the dust and cobwebs that make it impossible to identify the colour they had once been. The store has narrow aisles; its floor is so covered in dirt and dust that it's impossible to tell if the floor had once been carpet or something else. There are no signs that this particular building had been disturbed recently, maybe even since it was initially abandoned. I check the remaining stores and find them as undisturbed as the first. I walk back out of the store and onto the main road to wait for the others to return.

'Did anyone see any signs that anyone had been here?'

I ask once we are all standing together on the main road. There are murmurs of 'No' all around

'Nothing except a century worth of dust, it's like the town holds the world's largest dust collection,' says Ian, unable to keep his smart mouth shut

'Okay... Other than dust, did anybody find anything?' I ask again.

More murmurs of 'No' reach my ears.

'Very well then, we will stay here for the night, only for a few hours, though, we need to leave by first light.'

'Can I suggest that we find the least creepy and dirty building to stay in?' Skai asks me quietly.

'If you can find one, sure,' I say quietly, as we set off in search of a building to sleep in for the night.

We find refuge in a two-storey house that appears to be in better shape than the other abandoned buildings. We moved aside the rotting furniture in the lounge room of the house up against the walls of the room to allow more floor space; we agreed that it would be safest if we all slept in the one room. I ended up eating a small meal from my pack and washing it down with a few mouthfuls of water as a sad attempt of dinner. I was starving. The last meal I ate was breakfast. Both Ian and Lewis are already asleep the second that they closed their eyes, the others soon follow, and before long, it's only Ren, Harvey and me who's awake.

'You may as well try to get some sleep,' I say, looking between the two of them, 'both of you.'

'What about you? You're not going to sleep?' Harvey asks.

'No, I don't feel tired. Besides, you know I don't need as much sleep as other people do.' This was true, although, I was no longer sure if it was because I had trained my body so well at being able to function with little to no sleep or if it was because of the Genesi coding formula hidden in my veins. I felt as if I did not know who I truly was anymore, after finally learning the truth.

'I can stay up with you if you want me to,' Harvey offers.

'No, you need your sleep. Besides, I'll be fine.' I smile unconvincingly at him.

'Okay,' he reluctantly agrees, shuffling onto the floor and then onto his back to sleep. I stand and walk from the room, so that I can get some fresh air. The abandoned house is filled with dust and dirt that I swear I can taste every time I open my mouth. It is disgusting.

Once outside, I stand on the porch, or rather, what is left of it. I can tell that it used to be a wrap-around porch, but now, the wood is rotten in so many places that it has begun to collapse upon itself and the front of the house holds the only decent part left.

'Do you want to talk about it?' asks a familiar voice. I turn to find Ren standing behind me; I am surprised he had managed to sneak up on me. No one has ever been able to before. I must be truly exhausted. Or maybe I just don't care anymore.

'No, not really,' I reply quietly, so the others don't overhear. I walk over and sit down on the rotting front steps of the porch, and sigh. Ren quietly strides over and sits down alongside me.

'You know, it doesn't change anything,' he murmurs.

'What doesn't?'

'You being Genesi, or half-Genesi, whatever it is that makes you different from the rest of us. It doesn't change who you are.'

'How doesn't it?' I scoff.

'Well, you have been different your entire life, better than anyone else at what you can do. Finding out that it's because you're part Genesi doesn't change anything, you're still the same you, now, you just know why you are the way that you are.'

'I don't think that the rest of the world would see it that way.'

'Well, who says that they have to know? And besides, maybe you being part Genesi is what the world needs, someone capable of standing up to Chancellor Cain, to the senate. Maybe this is a good thing. Your father said that you could stop this war—what if you can?'

'I don't see how I am supposed to stop Cain. All my father said was that I needed to find the remaining Genesi, so if I do that, what then?'

'Who knows? Maybe they already have a plan. Maybe they can give you the information that you need to stop Cain, or maybe he intended for you to lead them.'

I snort. 'I highly doubt that.'

'Why is that so hard to believe?'

'Because,' I sigh, 'I'm just one person, just a girl. I would not know the first thing about leading people, much less, stopping a war.'

He leans in close to whisper in my ear. 'You might just surprise yourself then,' he says, winking at me.

I turn to face him, a retort already on the tip of my tongue and freeze. His face is mere centimetres from mine. I can feel his warm breath on my cheek; I can feel my heart hammering in my chest at the closeness of him. He leans forward.

'Did you know my father?' I blurt out. 'You know when he visited the base?' I ask, fidgeting with a lock of my hair to avoid making eye contact with him. I rub the lock of hair along my lips absent-mindedly as I stare ahead.

'I only met him once,' he says, leaning back. 'I must have been around eight or nine. He was nice, kind. You don't come across many people who are kind on the main base, especially towards me,' he says gently.

'Thank you.'

'I know you're not one to open up to anyone, I mean, aside from Harvey, of course. But do you mind if I ask you something?'

'Umm... sure' I reply, an unknown sense of panic seizing me.

'Is the reason you won't let yourself get close to anybody, open up to anybody, because of Harvey? Is there something between you two?'

I am taken back by his question. I give myself a moment to gather my thoughts and formulate a response that won't hurt Ren.

'Harvey is...' I sigh and decide to be honest, 'I have always known how Harvey feels about me, and I know that others can see it too. I guess I'm just not really sure how I feel about Harvey or about anyone for that matter. For the last ten years, I have really only been able to focus on one thing; finding my father's killer. I haven't had the time or the energy to waste on thinking about my future, and whether or not I will even have one after I find my father's killer.'

It was as truthful I could be without giving away too much. The truth was, I was not sure I would survive after finding my father's killer, and if I did somehow manage to survive, then what? How do I just move on from there? I didn't want to put Harvey through that kind of pain and suffering. I wanted him to find somebody that he can be happy with and have a future with. Somebody that wasn't damaged like me.

The sound of somebody clearing their throat brings me back to reality. I turn to see Harvey standing in the doorway; his face pulled into a tight mask to hide his emotions, something he usually did around others, not around me. Guilt floods my veins.

Shit. There was no chance he didn't hear that.

'Harvey, you're awake,' I say, jumping to my feet.

'Hard to sleep with the amount of noise the two of you were making, I came out here to ask you to keep it down,' he says, and stalks back inside. I scramble after him.

As I enter the lounge room, Harvey is already back on the floor, eyes closed.

'Harvey,' I whisper. He ignores me. Instead, he rolls from his back onto his side, so that his back is facing me.

I want to try to explain to Harvey the truth of why I can't return his feelings, tell him that I just want him to be happy and have a life, to have a future. I hope he can listen after he has slept, but some part of me knows that I hurt him too deeply for him to listen to me explain. But rather than talking to him, I lie down on the dust-covered floor, hoping that my head and my heart will be clearer in the morning.

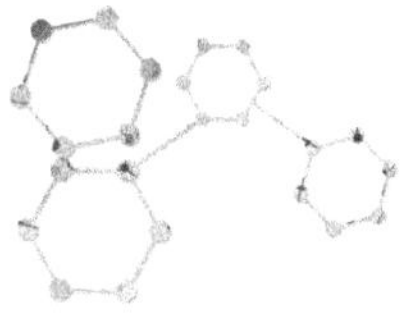

SEVENTEEN

I WAKE TO the sound of barking. My eyes fly open and I take in my surroundings. Walls with paint curling and peeling, a bumpy and warped ceiling, dust particles floating in the air in front of my face. Images of last night came flooding back, the ghost town, the abandoned house we crashed in, my talk with Ren, Harvey's face. I roll over onto my side and come face to face with Ren, his lips inches from mine.

'Morning,' he whispers, his voice husky with sleep and his warm breath tickles my cheek.

'Morning,' I breathe. Ren's face so close to mine is very distracting, but I remember that we are not alone in the room. I jump to my feet and begin brushing at the dirt and dust that has clung to my clothes. I bend to wake Harvey; I only have to place my hand on his shoulder before his eyes fly open. He looks away from me quickly—guilt stabs at me. I stand back up and take in the room around me for something to focus on.

'Would someone shut that damn dog up?' Ian mumbles as he rolls over on the floor.

I then remember the barking dog; I feel my stomach drop as I run outside to the porch with my knives in both my hands.

Both Ren and Captain Wells, no, *Liz*, I remember, are

already outside standing on the porch. They are staring at the road, no, they are staring at the dog that stands in the middle of the road, barking at the house.

The dog is tall and of a large breed, it has short brown fur with darker brown fur on its ears. It has a black nose and muzzle, and its lips are currently peeled back ready to growl. From this distance, I can see that the dog's fur is standing on end, it is tense, defensive.

'Do you know where it came from?' I whisper to the others.

'No,' Liz whispers back, 'I heard it barking, so I came outside, and it was just standing there, barking at the house. I didn't see it last night.'

Without taking my eye off the dog, I can see Harvey walking onto the porch out of the corner of my eye. Harvey has always had a soft spot for animals; he is such a compassionate person.

The dog stops barking. 'What's going on?' Harvey asks, while taking in the scene before him.

'We're not sure, this dog appeared out of nowhere and started barking at the house,' I say. I look both ways down the road, but I can see nothing that would suggest there was anybody else in this abandoned town aside from this dog and us.

Where did it come from? How had it survived out here on its own?

I turn back in time to see that Harvey is stepping off the porch and is now slowly approaching the dog. I tense and readjust my grip on my knives. He keeps his movements deliberately slow to show that he is no threat to the dog.

'Harvey... please, don't,' I call in a whisper.

Harvey ignores me. He does not stop or slow, instead he continues to advance on the dog until he is stopped right before it. I watch in horror as he kneels down on the ground until his face is level with the dog's face. I hold my breath as the dog's hackles lower and its tail begins to wag, slowly at first, then more quickly. Harvey cautiously raises his right hand and very carefully begins petting the dog, first on its back and then on its face, its tail wagging faster and faster with each pet until it jumps up and places both of its front paws on Harvey's shoulders, licking his face. I hear Harvey chuckle.

'O... kay,' says Ren, clearly confused by what was going on. *That makes two of us.*

Harvey stands as the dog jumps back down from his shoulders and he turns to the rest of us. 'It's all right, the dog is friendly,' he says, as he turns his attention back to the dog and continues petting it.

'We need to leave,' Liz calls suddenly, 'And soon. If this dog can survive out here, there is every chance that a human could as well. Or a Genesi.'

'Okay,' I answer as she leaves and strides back inside to inform the others.

With one last painful glance at Harvey and the dog, I turn and walk back inside.

I quickly find my pack and rummage through it until I find a small protein bar, sighing; this would have to do for breakfast. I tear open the packaging and take a tentative bite; it is bland and tasteless. It reminds me of cardboard. I chew the remainder of the bar as quickly as possible and wash it down with a few gulps of water, knowing that no matter how much water I drink, nothing would rid the taste of cardboard in my mouth.

By the time I finish eating, Harvey has come back inside for his pack, bypassing me and walking back outside. Probably going to share his food with the dog knowing him.

While the others are eating, I make my way outside in search of Harvey. As expected, he is sitting on the steps of the porch, feeding pieces of his protein bar to the dog. I smile to myself.

'Just could not help yourself, could you?'

He does not turn at my approach. 'You know me, my compassion is my weakness,' he says bitterly. I swallow the lump forming in my throat.

'Are we... okay?' I ask tentatively.

He scoffs. 'You tell me.'

'Well, you've been acting like you're mad at me since... since last night, so why don't you just come out and say what you want to say to me. I would feel better if we talked, or if you would just yell at me. Anything is better than you not talking to me.'

He explodes, leaping from the steps to stand in front of me, 'Of course I'm mad at you, you really don't get it, do you?' He is almost shouting now. 'For someone so intelligent, you are so incredibly naïve, Luka. I saw the two of you last night, heard what you said. I'm not blind—I see what's going on between you two. I see how differently you act when you're around him.'

I feel as if someone has punched me in the gut. How could I have been so stupid, so careless? Of course, Harvey was upset. If I had just thought of him first instead of myself, I would have known how he would have tried to read between the lines and misinterpret my words.

'You know,' he continues, 'all these years, I kept thinking that maybe one day, one day you might have the time for me. That you might have the time to think of something or someone else besides finding your father's killer.' He rakes a hand through his hair in frustration. 'For some reason, I thought that if you stopped thinking about your father long enough, you would see what's right in front of you, what's always been right in front of you, *me.* But you didn't. Instead, you saw *him.*' His voice breaks at the mention of Ren, and I realise, gut-wrenchingly, just how much I have hurt him. The lump in my throat is growing hard to swallow.

'I gave up my whole life to help you, Luka, I gave up *everything* for you. So, do you understand how I would feel, seeing the two of you together, seeing you confiding in him the way you never do with me? You have always kept part of yourself guarded against me. And, I always thought that if I stayed patient, that maybe one day you would let that last wall down around me. But, you didn't—not for me, you let that last wall down for *him.* It feels like I am an item that's served its purpose and then been discarded, tossed aside. That is how I felt last night.'

Tears burn my eyes, threatening to spill down my cheeks. My heart is racing and my body is burning with the warmth of shame at how much I have hurt him. I can't find the words to speak. What can I say? What can I do that will make this right?

'And you know what the worst part is,' he continues, 'is that I can see just how wrong he is for you. And, it's not because I am jealous,' he rolls his eyes. 'It's because you think he is this amazing person that you don't see all of his flaws, you don't see that the reason why you're so drawn to him is because he reminds you of yourself. You're a sucker for tortured souls and he has sucked you right in, Luka. He brings out the worst in you and you don't even realise it.'

I try to take deep breaths, but my breathing just comes out ragged as I choke back a sob.

'I'm in love with you, Luka, I have been in love with you my entire life.' He is struggling not to cry now and this pains me even more. 'And it's just hard to realise that you will never love me back, not in the way that I want you to, that I will only ever be your friend, nothing more. You have no *idea* how much that hurts.'

'I'm so sorry, Harvey,' I whisper through trembling lips.

'I know that you are, but that doesn't change anything, doesn't change what I heard last night or how I feel now.'

'Please, just let me explain,' I beg.

He runs a hand through his hair again, but doesn't say anything.

'It's not that I never stopped to think about how you might feel about me,' I said. 'I *have* thought about it.' My voice trembles and my breathing ragged, but I push through it. 'I have tried so hard for years to get you to realise that you deserve better.' I sigh. 'Harvey, deep down, you must know that I never planned on surviving. Even if I do manage to find my father's killer, the punishment for murder is death. Harvey, do you understand that there is no outcome where I survive to have a future? I never planned to. I didn't want you to have to go through that. I never wanted you to know that truth. I have always just wanted you to be happy, to find someone and have a future with them.'

'And so what? You just thought that I would one day wake up and just be over you? Move on? There is no getting over you, Luka. Where you go, I follow.'

'I never asked for that. I don't want you to follow me, Harvey, I want you to *live*.'

'That's not your decision to make, Luka!' he explodes.

'I know that it's not, and I'm sorry. I'm sorry that I hurt you, that I am still hurting you. But I need you to understand that there is no future for me. If I am going to stop this war, sacrifices need to be made.'

'What makes you think that you don't deserve a happy ending, Luka?' he asks, voice breaking slightly.

'Because,' I answer unable to meet his eye, 'happy endings are only for good people. I am not a good person, Harvey.'

'I don't believe that,' he responds stubbornly, 'you deserve a happy ending, Luka, that's all I have ever wanted for you in life.'

'I could say the same to you.'

Harvey, done listening to me, takes a deep breath and turns and walks back inside the house, leaving me alone as the pieces of me that he had held together for the last ten years shatter apart into a million tiny pieces, blown away by the wind.

The tears that had been threatening to spill break free and roll down my cheeks as a sob breaks through my chest. My tears burn my cheeks, it has been ten years since I last cried, and I feel everything I have kept so tightly bottled up spilling out of me.

My legs give out from under me, and the last thing I remember is collapsing onto the porch. I cry for Harvey and all of the pain I have caused him. I cry for my father. I cry for me.

Sometime later, I feel a hand on my shoulder, then I feel the hand move to my chin and lift my face. I stare face to face with Liz, the look of pity on her face makes me start crying again. I numbly feel her sit down beside me and wrap her arm around my shoulder. She holds me as I continue to sob into her chest.

'I'm not going to ask you to talk about it; I will make sure the others don't say anything to you about it either. When they finish packing everything, then we will set out to look for the entrance to the underground rail tracks. You can have ten minutes to get it all out, but then, I need you to be the soldier that you are.'

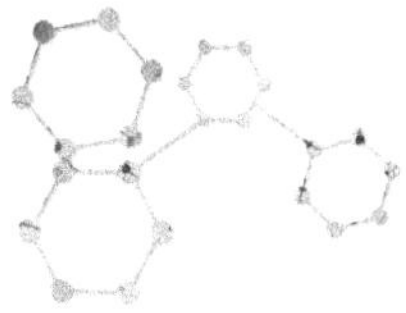

EIGHTEEN

SOMETIME LATER, LIZ instructs us all to pair up and span out to search for the underground entrance. I tag along with Ren as he searches for signs that could lead us underground, while my thoughts of my fight with Harvey run rampant inside my head.

We chose to walk back behind the abandoned houses to where the buildings are merely nothing more than piles of rubble. The others chose to follow the main road, hoping that it would lead them straight to the underground entrance. But, I knew that if the Genesi really were using the rail tunnels, they would not keep the entrance in plain sight for people like us to find.

'Do you want to talk about it?' Ren asks, breaking the silence and pulling me from my thoughts.

'No.'

He sighs. 'I get it, Luka; you don't have to explain it to me. I get that you love him.'

'What?' I breathe.

'I said, I get that you love him.'

'I don't love him... in that way, I mean,' I stammer.

'You can keep telling yourself that, but I think that deep down, a part of you loves him, in that way, and always will.'

'I... don't.' I shake my head.

'Luka, it's okay. You have known him your entire life; you have always been there for each other. You are a packaged deal; I can't have you without Harvey just like nobody could have Harvey without having you as well.'

'Can we please not talk about Harvey anymore?' tears burn my eyes.

'Sure, if that is what you want.'

'I just... I just need some time... to... figure things out.'

To figure out how to not hurt either of you.

'I can give you time.'

I keep walking, eyes scanning my surroundings to distract myself. There is little more than dirt and rubble. This side of the small town must have been affected by the bombings; there are no buildings left standing.

As we reach the last of the rubble and turn around to head back to the others, my eyes drift over to a particular pile of rubble that does not look like rubble at all. There are large sheets of metal roofing scattered in a pile, but unlike the other piles, this one contains nothing more than the metal sheeting. There is no dirt, no rocks, no rubbish or rubble from building structures.

'This way,' I call to Ren as I head towards the pile of metal. 'Can you help me move some of it?' I ask Ren.

'Sure, you think this could be something?'

'I think so,' I grunt at the weight of the sheet of metal I picked up. It was heavier than I expected.

'There is no way we will be able to move this whole thing by ourselves,' he says.

'We don't need to,' I say, 'we just need to move it enough to shine the flashlight down there to see if I am right, if I am, then we can go back and get the others, to help move the metal.'

'Okay then, together on three....one...two...three,' he grunts at the weight of the metal. It screeches against the other sheets as we slide it across, inch by inch.

We move the sheet just enough for me to be able to shine the flashlight and peer down into the darkness. I quickly grab the flashlight from my pack and crawl over to the small opening. I click on the light and shine it down into the small hole.

'I think I can see cement, possibly from a building or maybe it could be stairs. Wait.'

The light catches the reflection of something, possibly metal. I shine the light back on it and the light reflects again. Definitely metal. Stairs leading downwards, metal underground

'I think this is it, have a look and see.' I scramble to my feet and hand him the flashlight, stepping back.

I watch as Ren climbs down to the hole and peers in. After a minute, he climbs back to his feet.

'I think you are right. We should go back and get the others to help.'

We head back the way we came, towards the centre of the ghost town. My eyes continue to linger on the piles of rubble as we walk. As we walk around the remains of a building, I slam into something solid.

I stumble back and gasp. A man in military uniform stands in front of us. His eyes widen as the realisation dawns on his face and he raises his gun to my face.

Shit.

I snap out of my haze in time to react and knock his arm out of the way, and then kick him in the knee. He stumbles backwards, but recovers quickly, but not in time to see Ren as he smashes his head with a brick from the rubble, rendering the soldier unconscious.

'Where the hell did he come from?' he hisses dropping

the brick on the ground as if it were on fire.

'We need to find the others. There could be more of them,' I say as I take off running.

We run all the way back. My eyes search wildly for signs of any other soldiers. I slow down as we approach the last row of houses that I know will lead us straight to the main road. I creep silently along the side of a house, inching my way around until I can see the road. I see nothing to the left, but when I glance right, I stop dead. My breathing catches in my throat.

The others are lined up along the middle of the road, on their knees, a gun pointed to the back of each of their heads. And there, pacing in front of the others, is General Thorn. I quiet my breathing and try to focus on what he is saying.

'I am going to ask you once more,' I faintly hear General Thorn telling the others as he paces back and forth in front of them. 'Where is Luka Foster?'

My breath catches in my lungs and I almost choke on it. *Shit.*

I turn to look at Ren, only to see my horror reflected in his face. I turn back to the others.

'Do not think for one moment that I will hesitate to kill you. You are all deserters; death by my hands will be a mercy.' He stops pacing to stand in front of Harvey.

'Grab this one; he will lead us to her,' I hear him say to the officer that has the gun pointed at the back of Harvey's head. My blood boils.

I take a step forwards, only to be detained by Ren. He holds my wrist; his eyes are pleading, begging me not to go. I shake my head, telling him that I have no choice. I know that he understands. They have Harvey. Of course, I have to go.

I step around the house and raise my hands to show General Thorn that I am defenceless. His eyes widen at the sight of me approaching; he does not expect me to come so easily.

'Well, well, Miss Foster, glad to see that you have the common sense to know when you are defeated.' He sneers at me. 'Tell me, where is my son?'

'You said that you wanted me, not your son. So here I am.' I hope the fear does not show through my voice.

'Brave and foolish, just like your father,' he smirks, baiting me.

'Don't you dare say a word about my father,' I spit.

He chuckles. 'I stand corrected; at least, you give a little bit of a fight.'

My fists clench as I try to regain my composure. I can't lose control. Not here. Not in front of the general.

I close my eyes. *Breathe, Luka, in and out. In and out.* My eyes snap open.

'You said you wanted me, and I'm here, so what do you want from me?'

'If only it were that simple. You see... Chancellor Cain seems to believe that there is something special about you. He wants you back'—his eyes narrow—'and he will have you back.' He takes a step towards me just as the ear splitting sound of a gun firing erupts, narrowly missing the general.

Thorn chuckles. 'I take it that was a warning from my son not to touch you.'

'Perhaps you should heed his warning.'

'I don't take orders from my son,' he spits, as he signals for the officer who has a hold of Harvey to step forward.

Another shot fired, this time hitting the officer in the forehead. His lifeless body falls to the ground with a sickening thud.

Pandemonium ensues, and I use the surprise of the solder's death to my advantage as I charge to attack the general.

I collide with him, using as much force as possible to knock him off balance, but his reflexes are too fast and he plants his feet in time to take the brunt of my weight.

I feint right, then left before swinging my right fist and connecting with his face, smiling as this time he stumbles backward. He recovers too quickly and regains his balance before swinging at me, and this time, it's me dodging his blows.

Thorn is like a machine, throwing fist after fist towards me as he manoeuvres me away from the others. I close my eyes and focus. I can hear him laugh, but I ignore him as I slow my heartbeat and *concentrate*.

My eyes snap open and it is like everything is happening in slow motion. I can see his movements in time to anticipate his next move, giving me the advantage. I throw punch after kick at him, and soon, he is struggling to keep up with me. I kick his legs out from under him, and as he falls, my foot connects with his face, sending him reeling backwards onto his back and to the ground. I walk over and lean over his face. I can see his eyes rolling, trying to focus, and trying to stay conscious. I kick him twice more in the face until I am certain that he is out cold. Then I kick him twice more, just because I can.

I tear my eyes away from the general to gaze at the others around me. They are all fighting the remaining officers and losing. Several more officers must have heard the fighting as there are more officers now giving us the disadvantage. At some stage, Ren had joined in the fight as I can now see him taking on three officers. Make that two officers, as he knocks one out cold.

I scan the crowd until I find Harvey. He and Lewis are fighting back to back against three officers and they are struggling to gain any ground.

I race toward them and lunge myself at one of the officers, tackling him to the ground. We roll along the dirt until I am on top of him and my fingers are around his throat, suffocating him. His eyes widen in panic and his fingers frantically grab at my wrists, trying to pull my hands away. I grit my teeth and tighten my grip. When his eyes roll to the back of his head, I leap to my feet and lunge myself at the next officer, a red haze clouds my vision.

'Luka, that's enough,' Harvey calls to me, pulling me back to reality. I release the unconscious officer and climb to my feet.

I shake my head to rid the red haze covering my eyes and scan my surroundings. All of the officers are either unconscious or dead. I scan around to make sure that none of my unit have been killed or injured, and release a sigh when I see that everyone is fine.

'What happened?' I hear Harvey ask me, bringing me back to the present.

'What do you mean? You tell me what happened!' I yell.

'We were ambushed by General Thorn and his men. He was looking for you and then you showed up and then...'

'And then what?'

'And then you took on General Thorn by yourself... and won,' said Lewis in awe.

'So?' I huff.

'So, Luka, no one has ever won a fight against my father,' Ren adds. 'Not to mention how many officers you went through, you were like a blur.'

'A psychopath, more like it,' calls Ian.

I glower at him. 'I don't know what you are talking about. But, we need to get out of here remember, *before* they wake up.'

'Right,' says Ren, not missing a beat. 'We think we found

the underground entrance, but we will need everybody's help to be able to get down there.'

'Which way is it?' asks Liz.

'Not. So. Fast,' calls a voice. We all turn to find General Thorn climbing to his feet. His face is already showing signs of severe bruising. His nose is broken and possibly his left eye socket too.

I grab both daggers from my belt and twist them in my hands before planting my feet.

'Don't move,' I hear myself call. The red haze is coming back.

Thorn spits blood and smiles at me, his face twisted with malice. 'And what are you going to do?' he spits again. 'Kill me?'

'If that's what it takes.' *Please, don't let it come to that.*

He throws his head back as he laughs a deep, guttural laugh. But, I can hear the slight fear in it, just a hint, but it's there. I step towards him, daggers at the ready. I rush quickly until I am behind him, my daggers kissing his throat. Beads of blood bloom along his neck.

'On your knees,' I hiss into his ear.

'Well, isn't this poetic,' he drawls but complies.

I press the blades deeper into his flesh, drawing more blood.

'Luka,' Harvey warns. 'Please, let him go. You don't have to do this,' he pleads.

I risk a glance at Ren. He slowly nods, giving me permission to do what needs to be done. I swallow the bile rising in my throat.

'I'm sorry, Harvey,' I call quietly, as I drag the blades across the general's throat. His blood pours from his neck as he clutches at his throat, trying to hold it back together. He slumps forward, then drops to the ground. Dead. I can't look at the others. I wipe my knives on my pant legs and sheathe them.

No one speaks, so I take charge of the situation. I'll feel the weight of this moment later, once we are safe.

'Follow me, and hurry,' I say as I turn towards the row of houses at a sprint.

We make it back to the entrance with no time to waste, only stopping to instruct the others how to move the sheets of metal away from the entrance. Soon, we have cleared the entrance and I am standing, staring down into the darkness.

'So, who wants to venture into the creepy tunnel first?' Ian asks.

'I'll go first,' I say as I turn to look back at the others who nod their confirmation. I don't look at Harvey; I cannot bear to meet his eyes. Instead, I flick my flashlight on and descend the steps into the darkness.

* * *

WE WALK FOR three days straight. At least, what I can gather are three days. We follow the metal rail tracks towards the mountains, heading north and stopping only when we are too exhausted to continue and sleep.

For three days, I stay silent. For three days, I do not speak. I keep away from the others; I keep away from Harvey.

When we stop to rest for the fourth night since I killed General Thorn, I make sure to keep my distance from the others, sleeping as far from them as possible. As I eat the last few remains of the food from my pack, I keep my mind busy by estimating how much longer it would take us to reach the mountains. I estimate at least another half a day's walk, if not longer if I factored in how much slower we were all becoming due to the lack of food, water and sleep. I just have to hope that when we do reach the mountains and the Genesi, that we weren't killed on sight. There was no guarantee that we would not be meeting our end once we reached those mountains. And then that would mean that I risked their lives for nothing. I cannot bear the thought.

I hear the sound of gravel crunching; someone is walking over to me. I turn to see that it is Harvey. I say nothing; I do not know what to say to him anymore. I had thought of a million different apologies over the last three days, but none of them were ever good enough.

He sits down beside me and is silent for a long while.

'I'm sorry about what I said,' he finally speaks.

I half expected him to chastise me for killing General Thorn. Perhaps he still will.

I turn to face him. I am confused and don't know what to say. Eventually, I say, 'You're not the one that needs to apologise.'

'Yes, I do,' he says. 'It was unfair of me to say what I said, to unload all of my bottled-up emotions on you like that.'

'Harvey...' I begin

'No, let me finish,' he interrupts. 'It's unfair of me to expect you to be anything more than who you are and I realise that now. And I know that I would rather be in your life as just your friend than to not have you in my life at all because not having you in my life would hurt more than you dying. I need you in my life, Luka, even if that means having to see you with... with him. I can't lose you,' he breaks off.

'And you won't lose me, Harvey, not ever. Don't you get that?' I clasp his hand in mine. 'You are the only thing that has held me together all of these years, you are a part of me and I cannot lose that, I cannot lose you, Harvey.' Tears slide down my cheeks.

'You won't lose me, I promise,' he says. 'Where you go, I follow.'

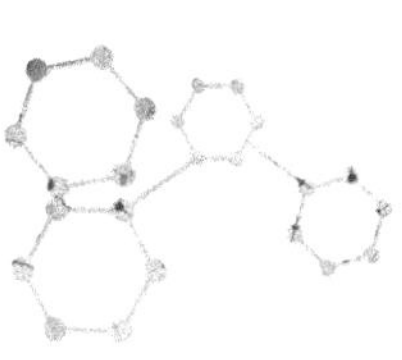

NINETEEN

I WAKE TO a hand clamped over my mouth. My eyes fly open and I stare into a set of unfamiliar eyes. They are pale blue and framed by dark lashes. The man's face is tanned from the sun and he had a dirty, scruffy beard that matches his hair.

As my eyes adjust, panic seizes me. Then I feel a cold pressure in the centre of my forehead. *A gun.* The man moves his gaze from mine and then back again before he speaks.

'On your feet,' his voice is gruff and aggressive. 'You move, you die.'

I nod my understanding and he slowly removes his hand from my mouth and stands, his gun still aimed at me. Slowly, I rise to my feet and take in my surroundings.

We are surrounded. I count two-dozen men, all with guns pointed at us. The others, it appears, had been woken in the same manner that I had been. We were all on our feet now, though it was clear that we all knew how vastly outnumbered we were and how pointless it would be for any of us to make a move against the Genesi. My gaze meets Harvey's and his eyes plead for me to not do anything reckless. I understand our situation well enough to know that we stood no chance against these Genesi.

A man steps forwards from the group of Genesi. He has

dark skin and no hair. He stands tall and is of a solid build. He holds a gun in his hands though he does not aim it at any of us. I estimate him to be roughly in his mid-thirties. In my analysis of him, he stands out as the man in charge of the group of Genesi who are holding us hostage.

The man in charge comes to stand before me. I can only stare up at him as his gaze traces every inch of me, assessing and committing the image of me to memory, the same way that I do. Then, he speaks, in a voice that is far gentler than I anticipated or expected.

'The dog, he tells me that you are the leader of this group,' his voice is gentle, almost kind, and it unnerves me.

He must have read my confusion for he clarifies. 'The dog smells your dominance. On the others, he smells their submission. He knows that you are the alpha in your group.'

The dog?

'I am not the leader,' I say, my voice hoarse, 'and I do not see how an animal could tell such things.'

The man in charge smiles at me, then laughs dryly. 'Pack animals are bred with a certain gene, which allows them to identify an alpha among subordinates. He can smell that while the others in your pack fear us, you do not. That makes you the alpha.'

'Because I'm not afraid?' I ask, bewildered.

'Among other things,' he smirks at me and I can think of nothing I want more than to smack that smirk off of his face. I refrain, but it takes all the self-control that I have left.

'How could a dog, an animal, possibly tell you all that?' I ask, still confused. I don't need to look over at the others to know that they are just as confused as I am.

'He is our perimeter guard, he warns us if humans get too close, but he led you here instead.'

'But he didn't lead us here, I did.'

'Are you sure?' he asks, mocking me and making me question myself.

'No, now I am just confused,' I confess.

'That's all right. I will take you to our commander and he can explain everything. After all, he has been expecting you.'

My heart stammers inside my chest.

'Your leader?'

'Yes, our leader, the commander of the Genesi,' he says, and smiles at me, causing the unease I felt earlier to return.

His words have the effect that he wanted because he could see that I was nervous now.

'And what of the rest of my... pack?' I ask quietly.

He laughed that dry, humourless laugh again. 'They will come with us to the mountains, to our tribe, but they will not be meeting our commander, only you will.'

'Why only me?' I question.

He sighs, 'I think you know why.'

I do.

'We won't be going anywhere with you unless you can guarantee our safety,' I say, as several of the Genesi laugh at my words.

'You do not get to make orders, Luka. All of you will come with us to the mountains. You—' he points at me—'will meet our commander, and the rest of your pack will serve as leverage. I need to make sure you don't try anything stupid.' His voice is still gentle, but I feel the full weight of his threat. The others would be held captive, while I was brought to their leader. If I tried anything, the others would be killed. Their lives depended on my actions.

Then it dawned on me: *he knew my name.*

My head was spinning. They knew who I was; they were expecting us. Was I leading my friends into a trap? I have no idea how to get us out of this mess, all I know is that we have no choice; we have to go with them because there are too many of them for me to fight.

'Very well then, we will go with you,' I say hesitantly, knowing that it wasn't really a choice.

The man in charge chuckled. 'Tie 'em up lads,' he calls to the others as they move to close in on us.

Out of the corner of my eye, I see both Harvey and Ren look to me, their eyes telling me that they would follow my orders. I shake my head at them, my eyes telling them to go along with it, for now at least while I come up with a plan.

We each end up with our hands tied behind our backs. My rope is secured so tightly that I can feel it cutting into my skin, chaffing my wrists. We are forced to carry our packs on our backs before our hands are tied, making our situation that much more humiliating and uncomfortable. We are separated by the men—Genesi, I had to keep reminding myself. I am placed at the front of the group and am guarded by the man in charge. The dog, the same dog from the other morning, also follows us, keeping close to Harvey, I notice.

We end up being led towards the mountains; a walk that I estimated only last night would be at least another half-day's walk. That gives me plenty of time to try and gather as much information as I can about the Genesi and their leader. The more information I know, the better chance I will have at getting us all out of this mess.

'So... how did you find us?' I ask the man in charge, trying my best to sound casual.

He is silent for so long that I did not think he would answer.

'We have access to your military's radio communications. A few days ago, we overheard that a young girl of significant value had escaped and taken several others with her, including one captain by the name of Wells. We knew that you would come looking for us, we have been waiting for you.'

I let the news of this sink in. 'So, what you said about the dog knowing that I was the leader, that was just a bunch of made-up crap then?' I ask, irritated.

'No, that much was true,' he chuckles.

'Did… did the radio communications mention anything else? Maybe that anyone was following us?'

'No one is after you, at least not anymore. So you can stop hoping to be rescued.' His voice is harsh. 'They said that you were important and they were searching for you, that every-one was searching for you. You were all labelled as deserters, but you… you were labelled as something else,' he whispers.

'What? What was I labelled?' I demand, unable to hide the panic rising in my voice.

He glances my way, but does not answer me, no matter how hard I push. With a resigned sigh, I decide to drop the subject.

'What's really going to happen when I meet your leader?' I ask instead.

The man in charge snorts. 'Do you really think I'm privy to that information?' he says. 'I will, however, warn you to keep you guard up around him; he has quite the temper and has been known to slit a man's throat if they so much as breathe too heavily.'

'I can handle myself,' I say stubbornly.

'Yes,' he says as he checks that my hands are still bound. 'You're doing an excellent job so far.'

'You speak as if you do not approve of your leader.'

'You could say that there are those of us that despise him, but I can assure you that I am not one of them. Most men fear him, for he has the strongest Genesi blood of us all.'

Strongest Genesi blood?

'Do you? Fear him, I mean.'

'It would be foolish not to.'

So, the leader of the Genesi is someone who has the strongest Genesi blood, which would mean that his DNA was not as diluted as others. Did that also mean that most of the Genesi in the mountains had diluted DNA, that would make them more human than Genesi? That meant that their lifestyle or breeding had to play a part in their DNA evolving? Was my father right?

'So... How come you have been in hiding this whole time? You seem more human than Genesi to me,' I ask tentatively.

'Do not be fooled so easily; we are masters of disguise. We have kept ourselves hidden all these years, even managed to infiltrate your cities.'

'*What?*' I stop dead in my tracks. The man in charge pushes me forwards to continue walking. I speed up my pace to keep up with him.

'Yes, we are inside your cities; our spies report information to us.' He smirks.

'How... how did you get inside our cities?'

'Now, why would I tell you that?' Once more, we lapse back into silence.

We walk in silence for several hours before we are stopped for a break. I am relieved to have my hands untied; they were becoming numb a few hours into our walk. I rub at them quickly, trying to get the feeling back.

I am handed an apple, as are the others, along with a few sips of water from a canteen. The water is surprisingly cool and crisp and I gulp it down greedily before it is torn from my hands by one of the Genesi and passed along. I turn my attention to eating my apple. I bite down into the apple and stifle a moan; I had almost forgotten how a good real food was, not the dehydrated packaged stuff we had been eating the last few days. My mouth fills with the delicious sweetness of the apple, and within a few minutes, I have eaten it all, including the core.

'We should get moving,' calls the man in charge, 'it will be at least another hour before we reach the exit.'

And within moments, my hands are re-tied, the rope cutting into the raw skin of my wrists again as we continue our walk.

The hour passes far quicker than I anticipate and we are stopped before a set of concrete steps. Sunlight pours down from aboveground as we ascend the steps. I have to squint until my sight adjusts to the harsh glare of the midday sun and I take in my surroundings.

We are close to the mountains now. I can see that there are in fact six mountains, two at the front and four at the back and a long valley down their midst. I can see the reflection of metal gleaming in the distance in the valley of the mountains.

'How much farther after we reach the mountains?' I ask, my anxiety getting the better of me.

'Not too far, we have to enter the mountain first,' the man in charge answers.

Within minutes, we have reached the mouth of the valley. The valley is much wider than I had expected. Two mountains loom over us, but it's impossible to tell the exact size of them from a distance, they are some ten thousand feet. The valley is filled with green grass and blooming flowers. I can even see trees and orchards. It is vastly different from the desert wasteland and the underground rail tunnels that we had spent our last few days trekking through.

We continue to be lead through the valley. Upon the walls of the mountains, I can see men—Genesi guards, I assume. They each have guns pointed directly at us, ready to shoot us down if necessary.

We walk through the blooming valley, approaching one of the mountains at the back. It is much, much larger than any of the other mountains. The closer we get to it, the better I can see the large archway that has been carved into the mouth of the mountain, forming a sort of doorway. There are more Genesi guards stationed at the mouth of the mountain, their guns pointed. The Genesi must live inside the mountains. I swallow my rising panic.

'Keep moving and follow my lead,' calls the man in charge as he moves to the front of our group. I watch as the Genesi guards move aside to let him pass through the doorway and into the darkness of the mountain. With one final glance at the sunshine outside, I move forward, through the doorway and into the dark depths of the mountain.

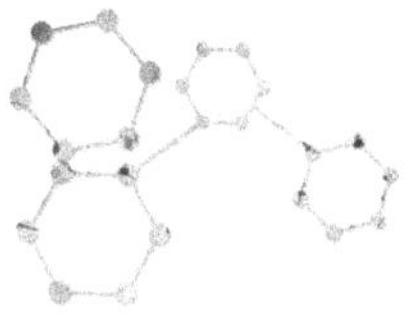

TWENTY

WE END UP being lead through a series of tunnels inside the mountain. The tunnel is dark and the temperature cold though it is a nice change from the heat of the midday sun. There is no light to illuminate our way through the tunnels, but thankfully, my eyes allow me to make out the vague outlines of the others around me. My friends would be practically blind. Despite my blurred vision, I would still have to rely on my other senses to learn the way out and commit every detail of this place to memory.

They lead us through several more tunnels that twist and turn and are all of a steep incline, meaning we were gaining ground, venturing above ground level. The twists and turns in the tunnels convince me that it is likely an attempt to confuse us, that way if we did attempt to escape, we would not be able to remember our way out again. *But I would.*

I make sure to take note of every twist and turn we take until I am satisfied that I can remember the right way out. *I will get us out of this mess.*

After two more lefts and one last right, we enter a large round cavern. It is a large circular room carved into what I could only assume was the heart of the mountain. The only illumination in the room is coming from the wooden torches that are placed around the walls of the stone room; they case the entire room in an eerie yellow-orange glow that flickers up the walls.

I can see several tunnels that branch off from the circular room and there, at the back of the room sits a single chair. *How bizarre.* The chair has been carved out of the stone of the mountain and is infused with sharp pieces of metal. It has a high back and wide arm rests and has a vague resemblance to a throne with large spikes. It suddenly dawns on me; this *is* a throne room, this is where I'll meet their leader.

I can hear a faint humming noise, almost insect-like. I look up in search of the insect and that's when I see it, *lights.* There are lights hidden up in the canopy of the mountain's ceiling. They are switched off, making it almost impossible to detect that they are there, but with my superior eyesight, I can faintly see them. It then occurs to me that the humming noise that I was searching for is coming from the lights. It is an electric hum that I can hear, which means that they have running electricity. *Why are they trying to keep their electricity a secret?*

I am guided forwards until I stand directly before the throne. I turn to catch Harvey's eye, his face betraying no emotion, set in a carefully controlled mask. I turn my head to gaze at the others one by one to see that they too have set their faces in a carefully controlled mask. Without even speaking, they had all decided on a plan, that they would appear brave, no matter what we faced, that they would not die as weak humans in the face of the Genesi.

I turn to face the throne again, schooling my features to take on the same mask as the others. *I will not show fear in the face of my enemy.*

The sound of approaching footsteps becomes audible to my advanced hearing and I cock my head to listen. Only one set of feet hitting the ground: *the Genesi leader.*

The man who enters the room is tall and of solid build, his muscles remarkably large. He wears what I think are black jeans, adorned with a long intricate leather jacket of sorts that looks a little worse for wear. He wears thick black boots and his hair is close-cropped, so that it is impossible to tell the colour in this lighting, it could be chocolate brown, it could be light brown or even a dark blonde for all I know. He is clean-shaven and has a strong, defined jaw. His lips are full and pressed together tightly as his face is set in a stony expression. I cannot gauge the colour of his eyes in this poor lighting, but I would not be surprised if they were black. He looks young, approximately twenty-five. Familiarity swirls inside my thoughts. I have seen this man before. *But where?*

When his eyes finally land on me, he smiles. It is not the kind of smile I was used to seeing on Harvey's face, no, this smile was full of malice and wickedness. He knew he had the advantage. He had us right where he wanted us. And he was relishing in it.

His eyes continue to rake in the rest of us, finally landing on Winston, eyes narrowing.

'Take his eye,' he barks at the others, his voice cool.

'Wait... what?' I say. 'Don't you *dare* touch him.'

The Genesi leader laughs, 'I don't doubt your abilities for a second, little Genesi, but this man here is a spy for your *Chancellor*,' he spits the word as if it is painful for him to say.

He thinks I'm Genesi.

'What do you mean he is a spy? How could he be? How could he possibly be communicating back to base,' Liz demands hysterically as three Genesi grab a hold on Winston and drag him on his knees before the Genesi leader.

'Oh, doesn't he?' he drawls and I want to smack that sneer off of his face, but instead choose to control my rapid beating heart. Then, I remember, he said to take his eye. *What is wrong with his eye?*

'His eye,' I breathe the question.

'Clever girl,' he motions for me to continue my realisation.

I think very carefully before speaking; I do not want to make a fool of myself in front of the Genesi leader. 'There is a biometric camera in his eye, isn't there?'

'Very good.'

'But how did you know? And how did we not?' I ask.

'Fortunately for you, I am much more familiar with your chancellor's methods, even more fortunate that his biometric configuration was disabled the second he descended the steps into the underground rail tunnels. No one knows that you are here, no one can follow you, no one can save you.'

That explains how we were ambushed so easily back at the ghost town and why they never followed us into the tunnels. They must have some form of advanced security technology preventing the camera in Winston's eye from corresponding back to base.

Out of the corner of my eye, I see him nod his head, a second before the Genesi guards holding Winston lock him into an iron grip. He tries to fight them off, but it is useless. I swallow the bile threatening to rise in my throat as I watch in horror as the Genesi leader steps forwards and grabs Winston's eye with his right hand, his nails biting into the soft flesh. I hear Winston scream in agony as his nails continue to gouge out his eye from its socket. Winston continues to scream and scream until finally, the Genesi leader manages to pull his eye from its socket and steps back. I hear the sounds of retching and I turn in time to witness Lewis, Skai and Ian vomiting on the stone floor—the acidic smell burns my nose. I turn my attention back to the horror show before me, swallowing my bile.

What is left of poor Winston's eye is a merciless socket that gushes red with blood. He collapses to the floor, passing out from the pain.

'You didn't have to do that,' I whisper. He ignores me and wipes his bloodied hand on a rag that a guard passes to him.

'Throw the rest in the cells,' he says, his voice dark and monotone, as if he were bored. 'I told you I only wish to see the girl,' he finished, as he strides towards his throne and sits heavily in it. His eyes bore into mine as the others are dragged from the room. I have no choice but to keep my eyes on the Genesi leader, knowing that if he catches me looking at any of them, then he will know that they could be used as leverage and I cannot allow that to happen. I struggle to hide my rising panic. I send a silent prayer to Harvey for forgiveness, for allowing him to be taken away from me.

Soon, I find myself standing alone in the throne room with the leader of the Genesi. His head is cocked slightly to the side, reminding me of a predator stalking its prey.

'What are you going to do to them?' I ask, keeping my voice as strong and steady as I can.

'For now? Nothing,' he answers in that same bored tone.

'And later?' I challenge.

His eyes light up as if realising something important.

'That depends.'

'On what?'

'On whether you agree to be my weapon.'

'Your *what*?'

'How about we start at the beginning first. I am Samyaza, thirteenth leader of the Genesi known as the commander.'

'Luka,' I answer his unasked question. Samyaza is an unusual name, and he is the thirteenth leader of the Genesi. Thirteen leaders in little over a century, that would mean the average ruling time of their leaders were about seven years.

It finally dawns on me.

'*You're* the chancellor's son?'

'Yes,' his slick smile fades.

'You're Genesi,' I stammer.

'Yes, though I thought that it was obvious, with me being their leader and all.'

'Is that supposed to be a joke? Are we telling jokes now?'

He opens his mouth to speak, then thinks better of it.

I stay silent, hoping he will explain further.

'I am second generation Genesi. My father,' he spits the words through clenched teeth, 'my father thought he had the perfect formula. Genesi able to be controlled. He experimented on me, his own son, and then sent me into the field to test his little experiment out.' He laughs, coldly. 'Turns out his experiment didn't work so well because his formula wasn't quite ready.' He laughs that same bitter laugh again.

'Your father… turned you into a Genesi?' I ask, both shocked and horrified.

'Yes, well, I did just explain that, didn't I? I suppose that we have that in common,' he drawls. I ignore his jab.

'But how did you become their leader?'

Samyaza sighs. 'The same way as my predecessors, the same as every other commander before me: I challenged the previous leader to a fight to the death. I won. Now, I'm their leader. So far, no one has been successful in taking my place.'

I feel nauseous and regret asking.

'Now, enough about me, let's talk about *you*.'

'What do you want to know?'

'Oh… everything, but let's start with the basics. How old are you?'

'Eighteen. How old are you?' I ask boldly. If he is going to try and get information out of me, I'll be damned if I was not going to try to get information out of him too.

He makes a noiseless laugh. 'Twenty-five, but you already know that,' he says. 'Now, stop playing games and tell me everything leading up to how you came to be inside my mountain. Best not leave anything out; I will know if you are lying.'

I clench my jaw. 'Fine. How far back would you like me to go?' I ask stubbornly.

'How about as far as you can remember.'

As far as I can remember. His words unearth the memories of the last few days.

'I guess it all started with my father,' I begin, 'He was a scientist and he worked for the senate on developing a cure for the Genes reversing the effects of the Genesi Coding. But, you already know that, because you know who I am, don't you?'

'I do.'

'How long have you been expecting me?'

I watch as he considers his options of exactly how much he should divulge.

'Since I first came here, about six years ago. I have been waiting for you,' he confesses, 'but before I tell you the rest of my story, I would like to hear yours.'

With a resigned sigh, I agree to his terms.

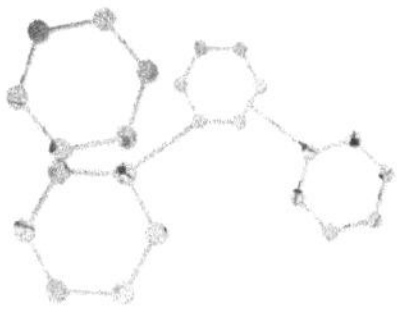

TWENTY-ONE

I TELL HIM everything, even though most of it he already knows; I don't leave anything out. I explain how my father was murdered, that I woke up with no memory and how I found my father's body. I tell him how Harvey and I trained for the past ten years, all so that we could be accepted into Delta Force. I explain in detail everything that happened after we arrived on the military base; my talk with Chancellor Cain and General Thorn, finding the video of my father, finding out that my father had hidden the formula for the Genesi Code in me, for which Samyaza did not seem at all surprised by. Finally, I tell him how we were caught, how we escaped and how we spent the last week trying desperately to find the Genesi encampment.

When I am done speaking, we stand in silence. I feel as if a huge weight had been taken off of my shoulders. If felt good to talk openly about everything that has happened, to finally let those walls down.

'So,' he finally breaks the silence. 'You don't know who it was that killed your father, and how far he came with developing the cure and the second generation formula?' he begins pacing the throne room.

'Yes,' I say hesitantly, unsure of where he was going.

'Interesting,' he says lazily, but I can tell he finds it more interesting than what he is letting on.

'How so?'

'Well,' he begins, 'your father's loss was broadcast nationally. I remember it as if it were yesterday. I also know that your father's death was the loss of any possible hope for a cure. The second-generation formula that was used on me is not the formula that your father developed. No, that formula was lost the day he died because he hid it somewhere. Somewhere no one was able to find it.' His gaze cut to me and I swallowed my unease.

'So how did you become a Genesi then?' I ask hesitantly.

'My father commissioned another captured Genesi to develop another version of the formula. Took him a few more years before he was able to test it out on me. Before I was turned, I had learned what my father intended to do with this formula. He made me into a Genesi because he thought that in my death, I would forget the truth.'

'But you do remember.'

'Yes I remember. He plans to raise an army of new generation Genesi soldiers. He plans to use these second generation Genesi to destroy the original remaining Genesi. Then, once that has been accomplished, he will demand that they destroy themselves to cover his tracks. As they are able to be controlled, it won't be an issue.'

'But you, you weren't able to be controlled.'

'Yes, the formula wasn't quite ready when it was tested on me and I was able to break free from his control while I was out in the field. Unfortunately, he has developed it since then and our spies report that it works phenomenally.'

'So, your father is using the recruits from Delta Force to raise an army of second generation Genesi that he can control, to hunt the remaining Genesi. And, once he has achieved that, he has commissioned that they self-destruct?'

'Yes, that is the gist of his plan.'

'So what does this have to do with me and my father?'

Samyaza starts pacing again. 'Your father was killed because he knew too much and he was becoming a threat, a liability. As for you, I think we both know the answer to why my father wants you.'

'So, why don't you tell me what you want from me then?' I am getting fed up. He is clearly playing games with me, and after watching Winston lose his eye, I am in no mood to play games. I want answers.

'I had thought that it was obvious.'

I wait for him to continue rather than bite at his ridiculous request from earlier

'You are the one that is going to decide who will win this war. You are the only *person* who is capable of proving that your chancellor is a fraud and corrupt, that he knows that the Genesi are no longer a threat, yet still wishes to go to war with us.'

The way that he says 'us' has me believing that I am included in his count.

'So... you want me to what? Blackmail the chancellor into stopping a war?'

'Don't be so naïve, of course, that is not what I am asking.'

'Then what are you asking? Just say it.'

'For the last five years, no soldiers have been deployed beyond your walls. We have been monitoring the soldier's deployment since your people built the walls that surround your cities, and only the last five years has it changed; they no longer come outside the walls. Until now.'

'So what does that mean then?' I ask.

'It means,' he says, 'that his army is almost ready. It means that he is testing them outside the walls, readying them for battle. And, now that you have escaped, he will be even more determined. His army will come for you.'

'So, what do you want me to do about it? How am I supposed to be your *weapon*?'

'Because, once you finally accept what you truly are, only then will you be able to stop this war. Even if they continue to create their own army of new Genesi, you're *different, special*. You're Genesi, yes that much is true, but you are also the biological daughter of the man who was single-handedly capable of re-creating the Genesi coding, something that has been lost to history. That makes you more than a soldier. That makes you a genius as well. You're more than just a Genesi, the Genesi coding is designed to enhance your mind and your body, if you were already a genius before you became a Genesi, you must be the smartest person alive now. You just need to learn to stop blocking it, stop trying to deny who you really are; then you will be able to use that incredible brain of yours to get inside and kill the chancellor.'

'You want me to kill the chancellor?'

'Yes.'

'Why? What good will that do? Kill him and another will take his place.'

'Perhaps so, but it depends on who that person is that takes his place.'

'You're referring to yourself. *You* want to take his place.'

His smile is full of malice.

'Why should I help you? The Genesi have destroyed our world, the chancellor just wants to get rid of them once and for all. How is that so wrong?'

His smile fades. 'I would have thought it obvious. Cain doesn't just plan to exterminate the Genesi with his new army, he wishes to use it to ensure that he remains in power. There is no need for him to start a war when he knows that we are not a threat. We have not been a threat for almost a century. He should be finding a way to cure us, not kill us. I want you to help me stop this war and stop my father. I want you to find a way for humans and Genesi to live together. I don't want my people to have to live in hiding anymore.'

'And how exactly am I supposed to do that?' I grit my teeth to prevent myself from lashing out.

'By becoming your true self. Once you start embracing your true Genesi nature, you will be indestructible and you will be able to find a way to save us all.'

Deep down, I know what he was saying was true; I just did not want to hear it. I have known deep down what I always was, I just refused to accept the truth, because why would I want to know that I am a monster? And now, now I do not want to face what I truly am any more than I did when I was a child. I want to keep living in the ignorance that I always had, but I know that I cannot anymore. I had to find a way to embrace what I truly was and find a way to stop this war, to stop Cain. I just don't know if I am ready for that yet.

'How do you think you died?' he asks me, throwing me off guard.

'I'm... not sure; I cannot remember that, remember?'

'I know you cannot remember, but did you ever stop to consider how it is that you might have died?'

'No,' I breathe. I know what he is doing; he is trying to make me face who I am, not giving me a choice to resist, knowing that my need for answers would get the better of me.

'I think I know. Tell me, when you woke up, was there any blood? Any wounds or marks on your body?'

I shake my head, unable to speak. The anxiety is coming. I can feel it creeping its way through my chest, like a hand grabbing hold of my heart. I start struggling to breathe, struggling to get air into my lungs. I try to suppress it.

'You were smothered to death,' he says matter-of-factly.

I numbly feel my legs give out from under me as my entire body begins heaving in an attempt to get air into my lungs and failing. I can feel the truth in his words as if I were living it all over again, and I am in a way. I can feel the panic and terror that I felt that day, as my body suffocated. I can feel the pressure on my lungs, the burning in my throat. Images start flashing through my mind, memories of that day.

'That pain that you're feeling is you reliving your death. I bet there are hundreds of others out there experiencing the same feeling that you are right now. There are hundreds of soldiers out there who have all been killed and turned into Genesi, all to serve your chancellor's army. You could stop it. No more have to suffer as you have.'

More memories begin to flicker in my mind, the hardness of the hand as it clamped over my mouth and nose cutting off my air supply while I look into the face of the man as he slowly takes my life from me. It was the face of a young General Thorn.

I feel the darkness take me.

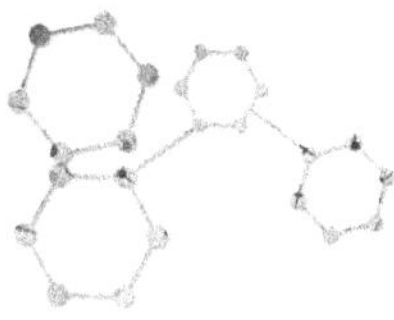

TWENTY-TWO

WHEN I COME to, I struggle to collect my thoughts. My mind is foggy with confusion. I shift through my memories of the last few days until I reach the memory of meeting the Genesi Leader, and finally, the memory of how I died. I was smothered to death by General Thorn, Ren's father. That explains why Ren felt so familiar when I first saw him; he looks like his father when his father was younger, when he killed me. I roll over and vomit the scarce remains of my stomach, unable to hold the sickness I feel at bay. I wipe at my mouth with the back of my hand.

There is every possibility that Ren's father is the one who had killed my father. He was there that day, and if he felt no remorse over killing an eight-year-old girl, there would have been no hesitation over killing my father in cold blood. There is no denying it; General Thorn had killed my father, then he had killed me. *Did Ren know?*

I killed General Thorn. Slit his throat when we were in the Ghost town. I killed my father's killer. I had my revenge. Why then, do I not feel any better?

And just like Samyaza predicted, the reason I suffer from the anxiety when talking about that day, the crippling suffocation that I feel. It's my mind trying to tell me what had happened to me, trying to make me remember. I should have listened, paid more attention to my memories instead of trying to block them out. If I had remembered sooner, I could have killed General Thorn on the first day, then all of this would have been over; I would have found peace. My friends would be safe—Harvey would be safe.

Do I even deserve to find peace?

And then, Samyaza's last words echo in my memories;

'That pain you're feeling is you reliving your death. I bet there are hundreds of others out there experiencing the same feeling that you are right now. There are hundreds of soldiers out there who have all been killed and turned into Genesi, all to serve your chancellor's army. You could stop it. No more have to suffer as you have.'

The pain I felt earlier, realising the truth, was excruciating. It was like I was reliving my death all over again. Sam said that there were hundreds experiencing the same pain as me. Does he mean that I could stop it? Is there a way to stop anyone from experiencing this pain?

If Cain really was building an army, and even if he managed to raise this army and terminate all of the remaining Genesi in the mountains, what then? Sam said that he was using his army as a way to stay in power. There would be so much death, and for what? What could he possibly gain from this war when he is already in power? And how can I protect the others? How can I keep Harvey safe, keep Ren safe?

It's time to open my eyes and face the truth, to face reality. Become who I truly am. Embrace being a Genesi.

I am lying down, my back sore, stiff and cold. I am lying on a stone floor, which means that I must still be inside the mountain. I can faintly hear somebody else's breathing, and as I turn my head to the side, I can faintly make out a figure sitting on the floor.

Slowly, I push myself up so that I am sitting up. I have

to wait a few moments for my vision to clear, my mind is still dizzy and I keep having flashes of memories distort my vision. I am in a small room made of stone or rock, definitely still inside the mountain. The doorway is blocked with big metal bars. This must be the cells that Sam was referring to earlier, the cells where the others were taken. Where Harvey and Ren were taken.

I turn my attention back to the figure outside my cell. The figure is illuminated by the glow of a torchlight. At first, I panic that it is Sam, but then as my focus clears, I see who the man is.

'Where am I?' I ask, my voice sounding croaky with misuse.

'Isn't it obvious?' he says in that same gentle tone that does not match his rough exterior.

'Fine,' I say to the man who is no longer the man in charge, I think I heard one of the others refer to him as Nate. 'How did I get here?'

'Commander called me in; you were unconscious on the floor, he asked me to bring you here and watch over you.'

'How long have I been here? How long was I... unconscious?'

'Almost a full day now, you didn't want to wake up from the looks of it.' He says lightly and I detect a slight twinge of guilt.

I have been unconscious for a whole day.

'Where are the others? Are they okay?' I demand.

'They are in their own cells, same as you, and they will stay there until you give your answer to the commander.'

'What answer?'

Nate loosed a heavy breath. 'Whether you are with us, or against us, remember now?'

I remembered. Sam wanted me to be his weapon.

'When can I see my friends?' I ask.

'You can't.'

'Why not?'

'Because you are a prisoner. You don't exactly get to make demands. You have twenty-four hours to give the commander your answer.'

'I'll see him now, on one condition.'

'And what is that?'

'I want to see *one* of my friends on the way. There's… there's something I need to say.'

'Fine,' he says after some deliberation. 'Get up.'

I scramble to my feet and instantly regret it as my vision begins to darken. I have to hold on to the stone wall for support until I can see again.

Nate opens the cell door with a loud creek and gestures for me to exit my cell.

I scurry out after him as he leads me down a long narrow hallway filled with empty cells. The cells soon become occupied as we walk further down the hallway. I pass the cells that hold Winston, Ian, Skai, Liz, Lewis and finally Harvey who jumps to his feet only to frown as I shake my head and walk to the last cell.

Ren, realising I was there, jumps to his feet and puts his face to the cell bars.

'Luka,' he breathes my name and I am almost undone. I take a deep breath and remind myself to be brave.

I look at him again, picturing the younger face of his father as he kills me. I shake my head to clear the painful memory.

'Your father,' I say loudly, loud enough for Harvey to hear in the next cell over. 'He was the one who killed my father and the one who killed me. I am Genesi because your father killed me,' I say with deliberate slowness as I register the shock on his face before all the colour drains from it. He never knew. *Good.*

I turn and walk away from him before he has the chance to say anything, I can hear him calling after me, but I keep walking, keeping my eyes on the floor as we leave the hallway and enter a new tunnel.

Nate leads me back to the throne room. I am not surprised to find that Sam is already there. He is seated on his throne, waiting for my arrival, smiling deviously.

'I am surprised you wanted to see me so soon, I'd have thought you would want time to decide your answer. I gave you twenty-four hours after all.' He says in that same bored tone as if he knew why I was here; he already knew my answer.

I take a deep breath and Sam holds up a hand to stop me. 'I have something for you. Something that I hope will help convince you to become my weapon.'

I had already made up my mind, but my curiosity got the better of me as I watch Sam motion for Nate to bring forth an object wrapped in a dark cloth. Sam strides over to Nate and whips away the cloth, revealing two small ebony black swords. I take a step closer to better examine them. They are small, narrow swords with curved pointed, prongs projecting from either sides of the handle. They are beautiful.

'What are they?' I ask in a whisper.

Sam smiles at my reaction, 'they are called twin sai, ancient weapons best used for short jabs to the solar plexus, something that I understand is your preferred fighting technique. They are yours, regardless of your decision. You deserve a weapon as elegant and lethal as yourself.'

With a deep sigh, I address Samyaza, the leader of the Genesi, their commander and make my decision.

'I will be your weapon.'